Song of the Deep

C.H. LYN

Horizon Publishing

Dedication

To the ones who still believe in magic.

Contents

CHAPTER ONE

An Unfortunate Engagement

Crown Prince Derek Montague Charles leBrock Douglas the Third preferred to be called Derek, so when he winced as the princess descended the grand staircase it was not at the first glimpse of his bride-to-be, rather the way he was announced.

Still, Lady Lydia Dumonte raised an eyebrow when she reached the bottom of the marble steps. Derek offered a polite incline of his head, held out his arm, and tried not to shiver as her slender, cold fingers rested against his wrist.

She was beautiful. Saying otherwise would be a lie. He was lucky, he knew it.

Her dark hair was twisted back into thick locks, half stacked atop her head in a natural crown, the other half cascading to her waist. Her pale ivory dress enhanced her midnight skin. Pearls dripped from her ears, collar, shoulders, and a tiara of them hung halfway down her forehead.

Her lips were frosted with opalescent gloss, fingernails painted to match.

He lifted her hand to his own, thin lips. The gentle brush across the top was accompanied with a tightening of her grip.

Without the time nor the privacy for any words the two turned and faced the crowd of onlookers. Derek inhaled. Slowly rolled back his shoulders and stood a little straighter as the members of Lady Lydia's court burst into applause. Her parents, High Viscount and Viscountess—the king's only family—clapped along politely. Her mother's eyes and cheeks were flushed and puffy.

Derek placed his left hand at the small of his back and, careful to avoid stepping on the Lady's flowing skirts, moved the two of them forward.

Her steps were stiff. As though his arm were a line, pulling her from the safety her feet found on the marble floor. Just behind them, her lady in waiting gripped the back of her dress and flicked it. The skirts shifted, giving Derek more room to walk. Lady Lydia also seemed more comfortable stepping forward with her handmaiden behind her.

Derek sucked in a breath. This was... an unfortunate way to start. He'd wanted a moment of time with her. Instead, their first meeting since they'd been betrothed—nearly a decade ago when they'd both been children—was in a room full of the elite members of her court.

Their welcome back to his kingdom would be much the same. He found a pinch of solace from the knowledge that they had a weeklong voyage across the sea before that happened.

Still, her unease clenched at his gut. This was to be his wife. His queen. Hopefully—one day—the love of his life.

He leaned in, crystal blue eyes meeting her glistening, nearly black ones. "Do you enjoy pearls? Or did they insist?" he murmured from the corner of his mouth.

Lady Lydia's eyes widened. She gave him a sidelong glance.

Derek gestured to the gold ruff around his neck. "For example," he continued, voice low as they passed a stout couple clenching the stems of their wineglasses. "I hate this thing. But the royal dresser insists. *Every* time."

Lady Lydia's gaze returned to the double doors at the far end of the hall. Their destination. Their exit from the palace and from her life to a carriage waiting to take them to the harbor. She didn't speak, but he noted a pull at the corner of her lips.

Her hand, still delicately placed on top of his, gave a brief squeeze.

Derek smiled. He turned to face the crowd, offering the required nods, thanks for a multitude of compliments and congratulations, and an occasional warning in the narrowing of his eyes as he passed one or more members of the court whom he knew to be actively working against his own kingdom.

They turned at the center of the room, swinging around to pass the royal dais that they might (once again) gain the blessing of the king. Lady Lydia's parents stood to the left of his high backed, sapphire and pearl embedded throne. Her mother, the king's sister, offered Derek a shallow nod before her gaze fixed on her daughter.

"Your Majesty." Derek bowed. "We come before you to humbly ask that you grace our approaching union before your, and Lady Lydia's, court."

Quick, memorized words. The king had been the one to offer Lydia up when Derek's father came asking. This was for show. Nothing Derek wasn't used to. Much of his life was for show, it was a part of his duty.

The king nodded, waving a hand about as he gesticulated on the joys of sending his niece off to marry the crown prince of an equally powerful kingdom to theirs. Derek kept his princely smile in place, chuckling at the right moments, and bowing respectfully at the end of the speech. His mind wandered. He'd heard the words before, yesterday, when they discussed verbiage that would not make either kingdom appear lesser.

With a final low bow from both Derek and Lydia (her a half-second behind him), they turned to go.

Her breath hitched.

Derek paused. With a glance at his future wife, he turned back to the king. "I might make an offer, with your leave, Your Majesty."

The king's wide nostrils flared. A glint of confusion flashed across his eyes, but he recovered quickly and nodded.

Derek turned his attention on the Viscountess. "Lady, it saddens me that my future mother is not due to attend our wedding. Might I extend an invitation for you to join us on our voyage?"

Lady Lydia's grip on his arm tightened. The tips of his fingers tingled as the blood flow was stemmed.

The Viscountess inhaled, a hand flying to her chest. She cast a glance at her husband before composing herself, offering a smile, and shaking her head. "I'm afraid I cannot be present for my daughter's wedding. There are matters of state to attend to."

Derek nodded. It was a unlikely, but worth a try as he averted his gaze from the tears threatening to fall from the woman's dark gaze.

He looked to Lady Lydia, also on the verge of tears and avidly avoiding looking at her family on the dais.

"Shall we, Lady Lydia?"

Her head bobbed in a jerky nod. With her handmaiden behind her they strode through the high wooden double doors, down the stone steps, and into the waiting carriage.

Derek settled onto the cushion of crushed black velvet across from his fiancé and her handmaiden, heaved a sigh, and tugged off his ruff.

It was going to be a long trip back home.

CHAPTER TWO

Biscuits and Bumbling

Lady Lydia spent the first two days of their voyage locked in her chambers. Derek did not pry or press. He insisted on bringing her the morning and evening meal but left her alone beyond that. As difficult as he found the situation, he understood the challenges she faced were immeasurably greater.

He was grateful on the third morning, as he approached her door with a tray of biscuits, jam, and hot tea, to see her stepping out of it. She'd opted away from the bucket-like gowns she'd worn the previous days. The design of this dress was simple. A blue skirt draped like petals, a charming cream-colored vest embroidered with matching blue flowers, and short heels.

Her hair was back, the locks held in a tail with a thick blue fabric. Tiny white flowers dotted the dark strands.

He smiled. A flash of heat drove through his chest, his stomach tightening. "Good morning, My Lady."

"Lydia, please."

Her voice. He nearly dropped the tray. Her previous words to him had been through the door. A thanks and apology, laced with tears he didn't mention. Now though... it was as if she sang to him. Sang with the mere words with a sound that struck a chord deep within him and brought something alive.

"Ly..." He cleared his throat. "Lydia it is then. And I shall be Derek."

She chuckled, a tinkling sound. Bells—no—birds. Not the shrill ones that woke you in the early hours of the morning. Deep ones, their tones haunting and beautiful at once.

"Have you eaten?"

Derek shook his head. "I wanted to bring you breakfast first, La—Lydia."

Her smile glinted in the dim light of morning coming through the mid-deck portholes. Bright and as true as he could imagine. If this was her putting on a polite show, he couldn't imagine how beautiful an honest smile would be.

"Please, come in."

Derek froze, his fingers clenched around the edges of the silver tray. "Umm." He glanced around.

The hall within the ship was empty. Sailors hustled around the deck above them, their footsteps audible as they worked to keep the ship on course while strong winds whipped at the sails.

Lydia laughed again, a mischievous sound this time. "My handmaiden waits for us."

Derek flushed. "Of course." He swallowed and stepped forward as she gestured for him to enter her chambers. "I've wanted to meet her."

"Lydia?"

The room was dark within. Portholes at the far end of the chamber let low light filter in. The lanterns were out.

"It's fine, Aly." Lydia's singsong voice filled the space. "It's my betrothed."

Derek couldn't help the wince. "What happened to just Derek?"

Lydia laughed. "You can set that there." She gestured to a petite round table in the far-right corner. To the left sat a bed nearly the size of his. A small cot lay at the foot, covered in cloth and furs.

Chests took up most of the rest of the space. Clothes, jewelry, weapons, and gold. Some possessions for Lydia, some for Derek, and most for his father.

Derek cleared his throat as he set down the tray and took up a spot to the side of the table, his hands folded behind his back. Nerves rumbled through his stomach. They weren't alone. Which was good, since the impropriety of such an action would result in disaster if they were caught.

At the same time the building anticipation of a solo conversation, let alone what he was expected to handle after the wedding...

He flushed.

"Will you sit with us?" Lydia sank into a chair at the far side of the table, dark gaze surveying him for a moment before she reached for a biscuit.

"I... Thank you." He joined her at the table. His eyes widened, and he leaned back as her handmaiden sat as well.

His shock only increased when the woman reached for a biscuit.

"This is Alyana," Lydia murmured. Her voice, the pitch lower still as she spoke in quiet tones, dimmed the ringing in his ears. "As we are to be..." She licked her lips and flashed a smile. "As we are to be wed, I thought it important that you understand she is not just my handmaiden. She is my closest friend."

Alyana's bright green eyes stared at him under her furrowed brow. She was as pale as her lady was dark. A thick section of red hair was braided down her back with smaller braided tendrils circled around it creating a pattern. Her dress was sage. Higher quality than the average servant, but nothing out of place for a handmaiden to royalty.

He glanced from her to Lydia and then nodded.

Lydia smiled again. "I thought, especially after your offer to my mother," she reached across the table and touched his pale skin with gentle fingers, "you'd understand my desire to have someone with me. Someone from home."

He nodded. "It certainly isn't outside the realms of propriety for you to bring a lady in waiting. Convenient," he said with an awkward chuckle. "That she also happens to be your friend."

He reached for a biscuit. Strawberry jam went onto the flaky bread, a healthy portion to compensate for his lack of a beverage—the tray only held two teacups. Derek busied himself with his first few bites.

The two women across from him ate. Lydia took dainty bites. Alyana finished her two halves in four mouthfuls.

"So," Derek broke the silence with a wry smile at Lydia. "*Do* you like pearls?"

Alyana snorted.

Lydia broke into a fit of giggles—distracting Derek entirely from his question as the sound flooded his soul—before she straightened and sighed. "I do. But not to *that* extent. The head piece was mine. The earrings, necklace, bracelets, and hair accessories were..." Her gaze met his eye for half a second. "*Insisted* upon by the king."

Derek nodded. "It certainly was a show of your kingdom's prized export."

Lydia's face fell. Her teacup shook against the saucer.

Derek looked from her to Alyana, lost and concerned. The lady in waiting glared, her fierce expression a harsh opposite of the wry smile that had been on her face only a moment before.

"She's not an *export*," Alyana growled through clenched teeth.

Derek's eyes widened. "No." He put his hands up, horrified. "Pearls. Your kingdom is known for their export of pearls. It was a clever way to bring attention to that for all the foreign dignitaries present. Ambassadors and the like." He swallowed and rose, wincing. "I'm terribly…"

Derek ran a hand through his hair, ruining the delicate wave he'd spent ten minutes working on that morning. "I should go. I'm sorry. I never meant…"

Alyana rose with him, walked him to the door, and shut it on his back.

Derek walked a few feet down the hall, his mind numb with embarrassment. He leaned against the wooden wall, tilted his head back, closed his eyes, and murmured, "That went well."

Chapter Three

Stars and Waves

T he sky was dark. Stars glittered above, their light reflected on the still water. The lack of wind had slowed their trip. Sailors would get back to willing every ounce of speed from the sails once morning came. For now, however, Derek enjoyed the peaceful deck in relative solitude.

"She's brave, you know?"

He jerked back from the rail he'd been leaning against. Heart thundering, he turned to find Alyana staring at him, arms crossed over her chest. She must have been barefoot under her skirts, to walk across the deck so silently. With an unsteady exhale, he nodded.

"I know. She'd have to be, agreeing to this." He gestured to the ocean before him, stopping just before he gestured to himself. His hand found the rail again.

His fiancé's handmaiden strode to the side of the ship and leaned her forearms on the decoratively carved wood. She stared out at the sea.

After a moment of silence, he turned as well and continued his examination of the stars. Another few minutes passed before Alyana spoke again.

"She didn't."

"What?" Derek glanced her way. A hint of a breeze caught the edge of her skirt. The light from the stars illuminated her pale skin, almost making her glow in the night.

"Lydia didn't agree to this." She turned to face him, her expression hard. "The king made his decision. She had no say in the matter."

Derek swallowed. "Ahh. That is... unfortunate to hear."

Alyana shrugged. She leaned her butt against the rail and crossed her arms again. "Could have been worse. She was relieved when we saw you."

"Really?" A spark of hope, or maybe pride, flitted into his chest.

Alyana nodded. "Oh yes. We've seen other suitors come and go. None are as young as you. And few had the..." She shook her hand at him. "Physicality you do."

Derek blushed.

"Not my cup of tea," Alyana continued with a curled up.

Derek's blush faded fast.

"But for what this is, you could be worse."

"Uh... thank you?" He blinked at her, befuddled by the entire conversation.

Silence fell again. He thought about leaving, returning to his rooms. But Alyana was close with Lydia. They'd made it clear she'd be around. He should get to know her as well if he wanted a relationship with his future wife.

"Thank you—"

"Her voice—"

They both spoke at the same time. Derek gave a deferential nod and motioned for her to go on.

Alyana cleared her throat. Her sure tone and steady inflection were gone; replaced with wavering. "Thank you for being so accepting of me. Not many are comfortable talking to servants in this way. It's one of the reasons Lydia feels lucky to have been sent with you." She chewed on her lower lip, avoiding his gaze.

Derek nodded, though he wasn't sure she saw it. "I've had friends of my own in the palace staff. Less and less as I grew older and needed to undertake my responsibilities as crown prince. Still, I see them here and there and I..." He hesitated, unsure why he was saying all this to—as she had just pointed out—a servant. "I miss them."

Quiet again. Less uncomfortable this time. Derek took the lack of tension in the air as a sign things were progressing the right direction.

"Her voice?" Alyana prompted after a moment or two.

"Indeed," Derek said with a wistful exhale. "I had no idea. Her beauty was described." He rolled his eyes and fiddled with the tip of his thumb nail. "As well as her family's wealth. But no one mentioned her voice. It's..."

"Magical?"

He inhaled and rubbed his hand across his chin. "I was going to say soothing, but I believe your word is more apt."

Alyana smiled. "Just wait till you hear her sing."

They chatted another few minutes. The conversation twisted away from Lydia and on to what the two women could expect when they reached Derek's kingdom. It wasn't long before Alyana excused herself with a low curtsey and promised to welcome him into Lydia's chambers for breakfast the next morning.

Derek remained on the deck another half hour or so before retiring to his own rooms. The clenched knot which had harried his stomach since he'd boarded the ship for Lydia's kingdom nearly three weeks ago, loosened.

Sleep found him quickly.

The next two days met Derek with surprising happiness. He, Lydia, and Alyana shared their meals together, always in Lydia's rooms. They strolled across the deck a few times, though his fiancé seemed—if possible—more uncomfortable in the open air than she did below. She confided to him that ships and the sea had always made her nervous. She couldn't swim.

Each time she spoke Derek was drawn in. The world around him faded when her melodic voice reached his ears. He wished, prayed, and hoped to hear her sing before they reached the bustle of his kingdom. Before the pressure of their nuptials interrupted the peace they'd found on the ship.

He didn't dare ask. It felt... too personal. Perhaps when they were wed. He'd already planned his gift for her. He might request a song for his.

Two days from their destination they were shuffled under deck in the midafternoon due to the rain pelting down on them. Alyana murmured that Lydia was feeling ill, so Derek found himself alone in his room. He attempted to read, but the swaying of his lantern gave him a headache. Even laying down became impossible with the force of the storm.

Almost two hours later the ship groaned and strained under the pressure of the waves. Derek slipped from his room, clenching the door as a burst of water slammed into the side of the ship, knocking everything sideways. He stumbled down the hall. Shouts sounded above him, pounding of boots on the deck. Sailors, trying to keep her steady.

He hesitated at the stairs. Lydia was surely anxious with this mess above them, but his priority had to be the entire ship, not one woman. Besides, she had Alyana beside her. He hurried to the deck to find the captain and see what he might do to help.

Above, a storm like nothing he'd seen raged around the ship. Wind ripped at his coat and nearly pulled him off his feet as he gripped a line of rope and clung to it.

He could barely see. Heavy drops pelted him hard, the cold rain stinging his face. He tightened his grip, planted his feet, and took slow but sure steps toward the wheel.

"Captain," he shouted.

At the helm, a stout man with a thick black beard and intense eyes glared at him. "Highness, you should be below," he shouted back.

Derek shook his head. "I'm not one to hide out a storm, Captain. How can I help?"

Something cracked. The sound pierced through the roaring of wind. Both men looked up. The main mast had splintered. Cracked in the middle. Though still upright, shards of wood stuck out like jagged teeth.

"Tie yerself to a lifeboat," the captain said. His gaze turned dark, shadows of fear flickering across his face. "This storm is one I haven't seen before. She's like to devour the ship."

Derek swallowed. His feet pounded the wooden deck as he ran for the door. Lydia and Alyana. They couldn't be below if there was a chance of the ship going down.

He reached the door, wrenched it open.

A roar at his back made him turn. Above him, twenty feet in the air...

He had just enough time to suck in a breath before the wave broke across the deck.

Chapter Four

When Water Burns

His lungs burned. Fiery and hot and painful even as cold numbed every inch of his body. He forced calm into his limbs. Into his mind.

Swimming was worth nothing if you didn't know what direction was up.

He waited. Let his body go limp underneath the raging waves. He rolled, spun a few times, and eventually steadied. He pursed his lips and released a small stream of air.

Derek followed the bubbles. Pushed up and up. Kicked. Pulled at the water with cupped hands. Pictured his mother's face at the surface, calling him up. Calling him to the breath waiting for him.

His head broke the surface, and he nearly choked on rain as he sucked in air. Screams filled the dark around him. He was still near the ship. Impossibly near the ship.

Though it could hardly be called a ship any longer.

The thing had broken in half. Shattered wood floated across the water around him. He flung a frozen arm over one, kicking forward. The lifeboats had begun to depart. He made steady progress toward one before another wave tipped it. Derek kicked harder, using his frozen fingers to paddle himself closer.

The men aboard thrashed against the water as one by one they slipped under. He reached them as the last disappeared under the surface.

With one hand clenching the edge of the board, Derek inhaled and ducked under. He stretched, reached toward the man sinking down and...

A pang of relief as fingers grasped his. He pulled, and the two of them broke the surface together. Derek yanked the sailor's hand to the plank, and they panted against the wood.

"There," Derek shouted over the wind. He pointed, almost lost his grip, and clenched their safety once again.

Closer to the wreckage, near the half of the ship currently sinking below the waves, three figures paddled a boat in their direction.

The two men kicked. Derek's legs ached as they fought against the storm. The let up in rain was a moment of relief but continued icy blasts of air set him into fits of shivers. His teeth chattered as he pushed and pushed and, eventually, reached the small boat.

Hands gripped the back of his coat and pulled him aboard. A few seconds later the sailor he'd saved collapsed on the floor of the boat beside him.

Derek heaved a few breaths, eyes closed as his heartbeat returned to a somewhat steady rate. Several seconds passed as his body continued to shiver, his mind frantically wondering if he could have done anything to stop this. After a moment he composed himself and opened his eyes.

Above him, a pair of wide, fearful green ones stared down at him.

"Where is she?"

Derek sat up. Alyana wrung her hands. Her fingertips were nearly blue with cold. The dress she wore, a simple emerald thing with gold embroidery, was as drenched as he was. Strands of red hair had escaped the braid and were plastered against her wet forehead and cheeks.

She didn't move away as he rose to his knees and found a bench to sit on.

"Highness." Her voice trembled, but not with the cold. Fear gripped him as he took in the other members on their little boat.

The second in command, a fierce woman with cropped hair and a glass eye, another sailor, and the one who had been with him in the water. And Alyana.

"Highness?"

Derek stared back at her, a wash of horror numbing him. He jerked, rising halfway to his feet before someone grabbed the tail of his coat and pulled him back down.

"Do *not* tip this little boat, your highness," the second in command, Ruth, growled.

He nodded. Staying on his bench, Derek scanned the wreckage. Waves buffeted their raft, but the majority of the storm seemed to have passed with the rain.

Gone were the twenty-foot waves. The wind had quieted. And yet...

Where were the other boats?

"There are six," he muttered, almost to himself. "Six lifeboats. She'll... she'll be on one." He glanced at Alyana.

"She was going to find you." Alyana's lips were barely parted. She clenched the side of the boat, staring across the water. "She was scared. Highness, she was so scared."

Tears burned at the corners of Derek's eyes. He scanned the water for another second. Then demanded an oar.

"What do you think you're doing?" Ruth snapped.

He ignored her, gave the other rowing man his shittiest princely glare, and started the work of getting them closer to the wreck.

"Where is she?" Alyana repeated as they moved through the wake of what had once been a ship. She rose to her knees, fingers white against the edge of the rowboat. "Prince Derek, where is she?"

The words came louder, angry now.

"I don't..." His chest tightened, heartbeat thundering in his ears. His fingers had gone blue on the oar. He dropped it into the boat as they reached the remaining half of the ship. The rest... the rest had already sunk.

"She has to be here." Alyana leaned over the side. Her voice was high, loud in the odd stillness following the storm.

"Stop her," Ruth said.

Derek reached out and gripped Alyana's wrist.

"What are you doing?" She glared at him, fury and fear and tears in her eyes.

"You can't go over. You'll drown."

"*How dare you*," she spat. She ripped from his grip. "She has to be here. We *have* to find her."

Derek moved as she did. Grabbed her around the arms and held on as she kicked, screaming to try to get overboard. The boat rocked.

Another sailor joined him. Pinned her legs to the ground as Derek shifted behind her and held her arms across her chest. She did not quiet for a long time.

It wasn't until the rest of the ship had dipped beneath the waves and even the clouds had blown away to reveal a smattering of stars, that her sobs faded into hitched breaths.

"How could you?" she murmured as he released her. She turned to him, eyes red and swollen, lips bloody from where she'd bitten them between screams.

He was silent. Staring at the water with tears in his eyes and a sharp weight on his heart.

"Your highness," Ruth said. Her voice was low but demanding.

He looked at her.

"Home is that way." She pointed up, traced a row of stars, and followed them to the horizon line. "With a steady sea and hands on the oars without rest we can make it by the end of day tomorrow."

Derek swallowed down the fear, pain, and regret. He nodded, carefully moved himself around Alyana, and took up one of the oars. The old sailor he'd rescued did the same and, without a word, they began the long trip back home.

She was falling.

No.

Sinking.

It was all cold here. Cold and dark but flickers of light showed where lightning flashed above the surface.

She was heavy. The weight of the dress, lighter than most but still pounds of fabric, pulled her. Thick pearls in a strand at her waist tugged her back to their home at the bottom of the sea.

Her lungs burned. The air in them fouled. Grew putrid and worthless and she let it out before it could choke her.

Her chest clenched with emptiness.

The dark around her grew; lighting faded into the distance as her vision shifted from crisp to blurred. Her mind shut down.

In its last, feeble attempt to keep her alive, her body over-road logic and attempted to breath. Salt burned her throat as water filled her lungs.

She choked. Wretched. Convulsed.

She gazed up as the edges of her vision went black. A figure...

Was it?

So hard to see in the water. In the dark.

Definitely something. Someone. Multiple creatures, or people—they had faces—swam into her fading view.

She reached out a hand, the heavy diamond on her finger glinted in a final lightning strike now so far above.

Everything went black.

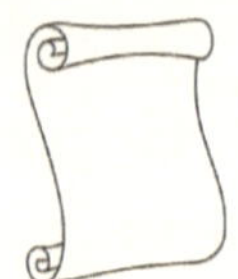

CHAPTER FIVE

The Old Tales

Derek stood in the hall of his family's palace. A structure which had been built by one of his ancestors and housed their royal line for nearly two-hundred years. Crystal shone from the windows, ceiling, and walls, everything in faded hues of gold and blue. Paintings decorated the long stretch of marble that led from the massive double doors to the throne room.

His father waited there. His father and the entire court waited to hear what he planned to do now. No bride. No dowery.

He was expected to pick another kingdom. Another princess to marry.

Beside him, Alyana stared at a painting on the wall. She hadn't spoken to him in three days. Not since Lydia had...

He swallowed and followed the handmaiden's gaze to the image on the wall. It was one of many portraits of his family and was his favorite.

Derek, the eldest child and heir to the throne, stood between his parents. His mother sat with the youngest, his baby sister, on her lap. His father stood, one hand on Derek's shoulder, his gaze stern yet proud as he stared outward. Children puddled around them, seven in total. Charles, barely two years younger than Derek, came up to his shoulder in this picture, though they were the same height now. His hair, dark to Derek's blonde, still flopped all over the place, same as it did in the painting.

"You don't have to come in," Derek murmured.

Alyana's sharp green gaze fixed on him. Her lip curled as the hint of tears magnified her eyes.

"I know…" Derek cleared his throat. "I know this is difficult for you. For us all."

She scoffed.

He glared. "It is. Whether you believe it or not, I wish…" He let out an angry breath and turned away from her. His hands clenched into fists at his side, a wince tightening the muscles in his back. He wished many things.

Wishing didn't make them so.

"It doesn't matter," he said. "My father wants to hear from you what you believe your king will do now. But I will make the necessary excuses if you want to leave."

"And go where?" she spat. The first words she'd spoken since her screams had turned to sobs on that little boat in the middle of the sea.

"I don't—"

"Derek!"

Derek whirled around at his brother's voice. Charles bolted toward them, moving with a pace that would have sent their governess into a fit. Behind him, a sailor jogged forward as well.

Derek frowned. He recognized the man.

"Charles, what—"

"Don't go in there," Charles huffed, pointing to the gold trimmed doors leading to the court. "Not yet. This man has been looking for you. He has something... you have to hear this, Derek."

Derek turned toward the sailor he'd saved. Thomas was the man's name. He was an older fellow, with greying hair and tired eyes. Still, he'd done his part helping them get home.

"Yer Highness," Thomas almost whispered. He glanced around, shifting on his feet as his gaze caught sight of the dozens of priceless decorations in the hall. "I know yer..." He swallowed. "I know yeh lost yer bride."

His gaze darted to Charles for a brief second. Derek's brother gave an encouraging nod, and Thomas continued.

"I wonder, Highness, if yer familiar with the Old Tales?"

Derek cocked his head. Beside him, Alyana had stepped toward the trio, a curious frown on her face.

"The legends?" Derek asked. He turned to Alyana. "Myths, children's stories of our kingdom."

"Aye." The sailor nodded. "Many *are* children's stories, Highness. But a few ring true. One..." He wrung his hat in his hands. "One true enough to be more. To be real."

"I don't follow." Derek glanced at his brother.

Charles put a hand on the sailor's shoulder. "I found Thomas at the palace gate. He wanted to give you his thanks for saving his life. He also wanted to tell you that Lady Lydia might not be gone for good."

Alyana's hand flew to Charles' arm, her fingers clenched around his sleeve. He looked at her, surprise on his face.

She spoke in a desperate hiss. "What do you mean?"

"Pardon me, miss," Thomas said. "There's a tale that explains why we don't commission many women on our ships."

The muscle just under her left eye twitched, but she merely gestured for him to continue.

"When a man dies at sea, he's lost. Gone forever, hopefully to a better place. When a woman dies... well, there's a bit of argument over what happens depending on how—"

"Thomas," Charles interrupted, not unkindly, "please, tell my brother what you told me at the gate."

Thomas shuffled a few steps closer to Derek and leaned in. "Highness, when a woman dies at sea, she... well, she becomes a mermaid. Left to swim the waves for all eternity."

Derek found a lump in his throat that stopped him from speaking. To scoff was his initial reaction, quickly stifled by twenty years of royal upbringing. Incredulity came next, but after that he found himself thinking back to the Old Tales his nursery maids used to tell him. Charles, being the closest in age, would have remembered them as well.

He caught his brother's eye, the same crystal blue that matched his own.

Between the two of them, Alyana had tears on her cheeks. She stepped forward and reached for Thomas's hands.

"You're certain. This is…" She sucked in a breath. "This is real?"

Derek moved around Alyana as heat flared in his chest. He took hold of his brother's arm. "What are you doing? You don't believe this—"

"I do," Charles said. "I've been at sea a few times more than you, brother. The sailors talk. Those stories we heard as children have real power on the water. I thought…" He hesitated, then put his hand on Derek's. "There's the cave on the shore where we used to picnic with mother."

A flash of dread went through Derek.

"I'm certain, miss," Thomas was saying to Alyana. "Saw it meself once, years ago now. Had a ship go down off the coast, closer to home than we were, so it weren't hard for most of us to reach safety. But…" His throat caught. "Marian didn't make it. I saw her, I did. Next night when I was sitting on the dock just starin' out. Wishin'. Wishin' never did nothin' for me. But I saw her, tail an' all. Real as I see you."

Derek stood frozen; Thomas's words echoed in the pitch of his mind as he reeled with information. As he pulled together a plan despite his reservations.

"Charles…"

"I know." His brother clapped a hand on his shoulder. "I've never seen you like this, Derek. Not since mother died. I know the Lady meant more to you than you'd ever tell father."

"It was only a few days but..." Derek clenched his jaw. "She was real, Charles. Real like a person, not a servant or a courtier or a princess. She spoke to me like... like *I* was real."

Charles nodded.

"I'm only going to see," Derek said. As the words left his mouth he was already walking back toward the double doors. Away from the throne room, the court, and his father. "I'll search out the cave, find out if mother's stories were true. If they are, I'll come back. We'll figure a way to rescue Lydia."

Alyana abandoned Thomas and rushed to Derek's side. "I'm coming too."

Derek shook his head, lengthening his strides. "No. It's too dangerous. Our mother," he glanced at Charles, "she warned of a sea witch in the caves along the coast. I won't risk your life for this."

Long fingers, stronger than he'd expected, grasped his arm. Alyana swung around to face him. Her eyes glinted with fire, fury. She inhaled through flared nostrils and let out the breath through trembling lips. "Your highness," she said with grit in her voice. "I cannot sit here and wait. She *is* my life. I am coming with you."

Derek opened his mouth.

"And," Alyana cut him off. "If you deny me this, I'll wait until you've left, find my own horse, and follow you."

Beside Derek, Charles snorted. Derek glared.

"She'll be safer with you than on her own," Charles said with half a shrug.

They'd reached the front double doors. Usually propped open to allow the salty sea air to refresh the interior of the palace, they were currently closed. Black cloth hung from their front panels. Matching drapes of black decorated every palace window and each of the spires. A mark of mourning for the future crown princess the kingdom had lost.

"What of father?" Derek murmured. He hesitated; one hand on the heavy wooden doors.

Charles cocked a smile. "I'll cover for you. Go. See if there's a chance to get her back."

Derek gave his brother a grateful nod, grabbed Alyana's hand, and pushed open the door.

Chapter Six

Road to Rescue

Alyana was an accomplished rider. Fortunate, as Derek had no desire to wait. They'd ran to the palace stables, fetched two steeds and a collection of supplies, dropped several gold pieces into the stable-boy's hand in exchange for his silence, and left.

Lagonia, the capital city of Derek's sprawling kingdom, sat on the coast with the palace as a glistening jewel in its center. Derek threw the hood of his traveling cloak up as they trotted through the city streets. The pace was agonizing until they passed through the fortified gate leading to the lowlands. There they found sprawling acres of farms and forests.

A wide, hardpacked dirt thoroughfare stretched south along the coast, hooked at the bottom of the kingdom, and rose north again on the eastern side of the mountains. Their stretch of road wouldn't take them that far.

They pushed the horses here. Open space, firm ground, and only a few hours between them and their destination.

After a while of cantering Derek pulled back on the reins. His horse was glistening with sweat.

Alyana raced past him, slowing a moment later and letting her horse rest while he caught up.

"What are you doing?" she demanded.

Derek frowned as he kicked up beside her. "The horses need a break. We're barely halfway there."

She shook her head and remained silent.

Derek let his horse set the pace, a moderate trudge. Half an hour or so, a break for water, and they'd be able to make it the rest of the way with speed. In the meantime, he took in the surroundings.

Derek had been outside the palace walls a hundred times. Outside the city walls too. Traveled on diplomatic missions, ventured to the great estates of the lords and ladies of his kingdom, even joined his father on a few hunting trips in the mountains that bisected their kingdom.

Never had he done so without a heavily armed escort.

This road... his gaze drifted across the reddish dirt for a long moment. Farmhouses rose up alongside them, small ones with one or two fields and a few chickens. Others were larger with sprawling ranches with herds of cattle, horses, donkeys, and goats.

He'd never seen them. Not like this, without men on either side of him, blocking his view with thick metal helms, flags demanding a bow for the crown prince, lances and swords ready to be drawn at the slightest threat.

A child waved, a basket of chicken seed in their hand as they jumped up and down on the other side of a low stone wall.

Derek waved back.

They stopped a few miles later. The road became a bridge, crossing a gently flowing creek. They dismounted on the far side, let their horses drink for a while, and then settled under a tree for a few minutes of quiet and ease on their bodies.

"I'm surprised," Alyana said.

Derek raised an eyebrow at her. She hadn't spoken since he'd slowed their pace.

She picked at a piece of bread. "Lydia was never allowed to leave like that. She'd never..." She sighed and popped a morsel in her mouth. "She'd never get past the gate."

Derek stifled a chuckle with the back of his hand. He nodded, cutting into a wedge of cheese and stacking it on his slice from their loaf. "I'm definitely *not* allowed to leave like that."

Alyana frowned. "Didn't seem like it was all that hard."

He swallowed, a weight settling in his chest. "My uh... my personal guard went down with the ship."

Alyana's pale complexion went a little green.

He looked away from her, out at the open fields before them. In the distance, small as ants, farmers tended to crops, herded cattle this way and that, mended fences, and went about their lives.

"When I was young, when my mother was alive, we left the palace often. Always with the royal escort, of course, but we explored everything within a day of Lagonia. Anything longer and we needed more men, more supplies, my father's explicit permission." He gave a bitter grin. "When she died, I wanted to see it all again. Our special places. The bakery where the owner called mother by her name. The tavern she convinced the guards to take a break in while we picked out clothes in the market."

The muscles in his cheeks relaxed as memory and nostalgia encompassed him. He leaned against the tree, rolling a grape around in his fingers.

"There's a little inn, a few miles east of the city that makes the most delicious hot chocolate you've ever tasted. And the shore..." He glanced south, down the road they would take up again soon. "I wanted to go back to see all those things. See my kingdom as a person rather than a station. One last time, maybe. At the least once more with my brother." He fell quiet, popping the grape into his mouth and chewing slowly.

"Did you?" Alyana asked, her intense eyes fixed on him.

Derek gave a rueful smile. "No. We tried to leave a few weeks after her funeral, but the guards wouldn't let me past the gate. I gave it half a dozen attempts, but even with a full escort..." He shook his head. "My father didn't want his crown prince in the real world. Better to keep me in the palace. Keep me safe."

"Charles said he's been on the sea more than you?"

Derek nodded. "He's not next in line. He and my other siblings have more freedom to explore our kingdom and our shores than I do."

Alyana frowned. "Why today then? Why did they let you through the gates?"

Derek laughed as he rose to his feet, dusting off his riding pants and packing up the rest of their food. "I don't think *let* is the word. I haven't tried to leave on my own since I was fourteen." He shrugged. "That, combined with a delay in finding a new personal guard for the crown prince..."

"I see." Alyana tucked her things into her saddle bag. She looped a small, sheathed dagger onto her belt. "And when we return to the palace?"

Derek's smile fell. He shook off the chill that ran down his spine and hefted himself onto his horse. "I hadn't thought of that." He swallowed. "I imagine I won't be allowed to leave the palace grounds for some time."

"If the tales are true..." Alyana climbed atop her horse as well, gripped the reins in her gloved hands, and turned them back toward the road. "How will we get to her if you're stuck inside the palace?"

Derek clicked his horse into a trot.

Alyana caught up to him, and they rode side by side for a while.

Eventually, Derek answered her question. His voice shook somewhat as he straightened in his saddle and glanced at her. "I suppose, if there is a chance to rescue her, we'll have to do that before we go back."

"And your father?"

Derek stared down the road, toward the sea cliffs in the distance. "I'll deal with that when the time comes."

CHAPTER SEVEN

A Prince and A Peasant

They left the horses at an inn a mile or so from the shore and walked the rest of the way. Alyana hiked up her skirt as they drudged down an overgrown dirt path that quickly turned to sand.

"The *queen* took you here?" Alyana asked, an eyebrow arched and incredulity in her voice.

Derek glanced back and then followed her gaze to the buildup of seaweed, driftwood, and shells littering the beach. He grinned. "She never liked the shores hear Lagonia. They're always so crowded."

Alyana's shoe squelched into something rubbery. She groaned.

"Besides," Derek continued, slowing to wait for her before pointing just past the edge of the water, "they don't have this kind of view."

"Oh..."

He smiled as her gaze caught the image before them.

At the edge of the surf, just past where the little one-foot-tall waves broke, was a gnarled set of rocky structures. Twisted like hands overlapping each other, with barnacles, coral, starfish, and a hundred more salty creatures stuck to the jagged sides. It stretched at least a hundred feet into the deep, towering nearly thirty feet high. The waterline cut the thing in half. In low tide, the bottom was still dark with life. The top had paled in the sun and served as home to a plethora of birds squawking and pecking as Derek and Alyana drew nearer to the surf.

"It's beautiful."

Derek nodded. "I hoped you'd think so." There was tension in his tone.

Alyana glanced at him. She looked back at the structure. Derek sighed.

"We're going in there?" she demanded, one hand flopping toward it rather limply before it fell to her side again.

Another nod. "That's where..." Derek ran a hand through his hair, chest warming with embarrassment. "This feels so stupid. Childish."

"What does?"

"This." Derek kicked a driftwood stick and it flew into the sea. "This whole notion of Old Tales, and sea witches, and—"

"Say that again?" Alyana interrupted; her eyes wide as she turned to him. "Sea witches?"

Derek puffed a breath out through pursed lips. "My mother brought us here often, and while we were allowed to play wherever we wished along the beach," he gestured to the mile of coast that stretched north and south of where they stood, "we were never to go near *this*." He pointed to the rock hands. "Eventually, my brother and I asked why."

Alyana brushed a strand of red from her face. She studied the formation with squinted eyes. "And?"

"She told us later that night after the little ones had gone to bed. Legend, and apparently reports from the local villagers, say a sea witch lives there. One who has power over the ocean and the tides. One who has no mercy for adults and children alike. No mercy for humans. She cares only for power."

Alyana gulped.

Derek took a step toward the water and Alyana followed. "She likes making deals, apparently. We got reports when I was child, of a disturbing old woman venturing into the villages in this area and offering beautiful bounties of treasure, youth, power, in exchange for horrible rewards."

She glanced at him. "Do I want to know?"

"The one my mother told us about involved trading an infant for a chest of gold. Obviously, the villagers turned her down, but still..."

"I don't have anything to trade, Derek." Alyana's gaze met his for a brief moment. "Everything I had went down in that ship."

He nodded. "Crown prince, remember? I'll have something she wants, I'm sure of it." He hesitated. "If... you understand this may all be myth. We might find nothing but fish and sand in those caves."

The muscle along Alyana's jaw tightened. She swallowed and gave a sharp nod.

The water was cold. Frigid and strong against Derek's ankles, then shins, then knees as they waded toward a shadowed arch in the side of the rock. It was on the far side of the beach, impossible to see from the shore, but Derek had been out on the water in his youth. They'd fished along this strip of beach. His mother had taught him how to thread the line.

"Delicate fingers, Derek. Like embroidery or sewing."

"Princes don't sew, Mama."

"Well!" She'd laughed then, raucous and loud and not at all proper for a queen. *"If you keep coming home with holes in your clothes you'll have to learn."*

"Derek?" Alyana's voice broke through the memory. Her hand was out, reaching for his as the water pummeled their thighs.

He took it and helped her catch up to him. She kept a tight grip as they reached the entrance.

The water shifted as they took the first few steps into the darkness. Light was swallowed here. Eaten by the shifting waves, shifting shadows. Ahead was nothing but black. Derek moved himself a little in front of Alyana, hand tight around hers as he kept her behind him.

"Slow," he murmured. "I don't want to startle anything."

He moved his right hand—the free hand—towards the hilt of his sword. A short thing, meant for quick defense and sparing, not full combat. His steps were cautious. The ground beneath them tilted, angling up until they stepped from the water, their boots squelching against a thin layer of sand over a rocky floor.

"I can't see," Alyana whispered.

As the words left her mouth, a flame of green light erupted in the darkness ahead of them.

Voices echoed through the cave, shrill and deep and trembling all at once. "*A prince and a peasant entered a cave... must be so brave, to enter the cave...*" The words sounded like a song.

Derek's heartbeat thundered in his ears, barely a whisper next to the volume of the voices.

They quieted, somewhat, as they sang out again. "*They entered a cave... Might be their grave? Why, oh why, would they enter the cave?*"

Alyana's hand tightened around his, and he heard the unmistakable draw of a dagger behind him.

"Calm," he said through barely opened lips.

Her hand shook in his.

The fire ahead of them shrank. As the blinding light dimmed, the features of the cavern they'd entered became visible.

"*A prince and a peasant entered a cave.*" The voice went quieter still, becoming one rather than many. A feminine voice, lilting and melodic. "*Who must they save, to have entered the cave?*"

Derek swallowed.

Through the shadows created by the flickering flame, a figure stepped toward them.

Chapter Eight

The Witch

Shadows clung to the witch. Whisps of darkness streamed off her like smoke, but it wasn't. The green fire roaring in a circle of stones in the center of the cavern gave off no smoke nor scent.

Derek's gaze stuck on the creature moving toward them. Her head was tilted at an odd angle, bright yellow eyes studied him from tip to toe. He kept his hand steady at his hilt, not making a move to draw but not relaxing either.

She was shorter than him, bent and hooked, but her face didn't look like what he'd imagined as a child. Her skin was a soft brown, smooth except for spiderweb-like cracks of black along her forehead and jaw. As though she were made of some hard material, hard and fragile that something had struck. A dropped vase that had yet to shatter completely.

A crown of coral, and what he hoped was driftwood but could have easily been bone, sat nestled in her stringy black hair.

She took another step closer, bare feet on the rough rock. Her clothes, a dress draped across one shoulder and ending just past her knees, appeared to be made of a discarded sail. One hand rose, darkened fingernails almost an inch long and sharpened, and reached toward Derek's face.

He gulped. Alyana's grip tightened but he squeezed back, hoping the motion would keep her from acting just yet.

The sea witch leaned in and drew a fingernail down Derek's cheek. The touch was soft. It sent a chill down his spine, fear holding tight to his lungs, but he did not move.

Her hand darted back. The curious expression on her face split into a wide grin. Sharp, pointed teeth gleamed as she backed up again and let out a cackle.

"Welcome!"

Derek released his breath. He did not remove his hand from his hilt. "Thank you." He cleared his throat. "I... we have come seeking the sea witch."

"Yes, yes, yes." The woman—witch—thing—scurried around the fire with surprising speed. "A prince and a peasant went into the cave..." She rounded the far side and sped back toward them.

Derek's fingers tightened around his sword as she stopped a few inches from Alyana.

The witch squinted. "Peasant?" She pursed her lips and clicked her tongue. "No. Prince and lady?"

Alyana swallowed, one hand holding Derek's, the other white as bone around her dagger hilt. "Not a lady. Hand-maiden, at best." She cracked a nervous smile.

The witch paused, blinked, and leaned back with a roar of laughter. It echoed through the cave, shooting another burst of nerves up Derek's spine. "Handmaiden. Too much. Too long. You'll be the lady and I'll be the witch and he'll be the prince and we will tell such a story!" She whirled, throwing her hands into the air, and spinning back toward the fire.

She stared at them, her chin just above the flames. "I do love a good story."

Derek stepped forward. Alyana's breath hitched, but she followed him.

"What may we call you?" Derek asked.

The witch frowned. "I'm the witch."

He nodded and gave half a shrug. "And I'm the prince, but I do prefer to be called Derek."

There was a pause during which Derek glanced around. The dark walls, similar in color to the low exterior of the caves but dry, glinted faintly with the green light. Make-shift shelves, halved chunks of driftwood and ship planks, were lined with an array of curious objects. Vials of liquids, bunches of seaweed, small skeletons, what looked like pickled eels... Derek stopped examining the walls.

"I'm Alyana," Alyana said as she stepped forward. She released Derek's hand, crossing to look at a silver box on one of the shelves.

"Hmm..." The witch scratched at her smooth chin with one long nail. "Florance? No... Epoidia?" She scowled. "That doesn't roll off the teeth at all. I had a name..." Her gaze went wide, arcing across the ceiling as a long pause drew a line of tension into the cavern.

"You like to make deals?" Alyana murmured. She'd reached a shelf of scrolls, stacked high between two towering candles. "Trades? Pacts?"

Derek's hand tightened once again on his hilt as the witch scurried around the fire toward Alyana. She stopped a few feet away, head at that odd angle, and showed her teeth.

"Indeed."

"In my language, we called that symphonia. How does that sound on your..." She raised an eyebrow. "Teeth?"

"Symphonia..." The witch's wide smile went wider still.

Derek was almost worried the cracks in her skin might deepen.

"I like it. You will be Alyana, you will be Derek," she pointed at each of them, "and I will be Symphonia."

Derek exhaled a breath of relief. "Excellent, now we've got the pleasantries out of the way, Miss Symphonia... we have a few questions."

CHAPTER NINE

Two for the Price of Two

"Well, of course it's true." The witch, newly named Symphonia, scoffed. With a flick of her hand the fire grew again, warming the cool interior of her cavern.

Alyana murmured her thanks and scooted closer to the flames. She already sat near enough to dry the hem of her dress, perched on a thick stump of driftwood.

Derek spluttered at the witch's casual manor. "She's alive then? Lady Lydia isn't lost?"

Symphonia cackled. The sound echoed through the interior of the rock walls. "Never said she wasn't *lost*. Everything dear has a cost," she said in a singsong voice. Then she gave a quick jerk of her head and blinked. "Not quite, prince. I said the Old Tale you speak of is true. A woman who dies at sea turns into... something else." She gave a crooked, toothy sneer.

"What do you mean, something else?" Alyana asked, urgent concern in her tone. "She'll still be Lydia, won't she?"

"That gets tricky. It depends on how she died."

Derek swallowed, an ache cutting through his gut at the thought of all those who'd drowned on their voyage across the sea. "She drowned. They all..." He inhaled through his nose. "They all drowned."

Symphonia nodded. "I figured as much." She heaved a sigh. "If a woman dies a natural death, she becomes a mermaid. Swimming the sea with her sisters for all eternity. Free." Her gaze flicked to Alyana.

The handmaiden watched the witch with a locked jaw, her hands tight at her sides.

"Some women prefer that freedom." Symphonia looked to Derek. "However, if it wasn't natural. If she was killed. If it was violent, malicious... That is when a woman becomes something different."

"What?" Derek asked, a curious furrow in his brow.

"A siren," Alyana uttered through gritted teeth.

Derek stared. "How do you know?"

"We have a similar legend in our kingdom." She gazed at the flames; her expression marred with anger. "Yours might limit the number of women on ships, ours outlaws their presence on the sea at all."

Derek's brow furrowed. His chest sank at the thought of an entire kingdom outlawing women from sailing. "I didn't know that about your kingdom."

She ignored him and looked at Symphonia. "It wasn't violent. But... if her state of mind mattered—"

"It mattered," Symphonia cut across. "It always matters. Why?" Another grin, a crooked smirk that showed too many of her jagged teeth. "Was she scared? Angry? Craving blood? Revenge?"

Derek's eyes widened with alarm. He glanced at Alyana, inching slightly away from the sea witch.

"I don't know about the last two," Alyana murmured. "But she was absolutely scared." She swallowed. "And we were both angry."

Derek opened his mouth, but a stirring in his gut told him to hold the question until later. Until he could ask Alyana without a sea witch present.

"Well," he clapped his hands together and stepped forward, "now we know she's not dead. How do we get her back?"

"Assuming you could provide something worth the trade..." Symphonia moved toward him, surprisingly smooth as she stepped across the sharp rocks with her bare feet. She stood at his shoulder, the tip of her shell and bone crown just below his eye. "I might be able to help you find her. Do you think you can cover the cost, prince?"

Derek straightened, putting another half inch between their heights, and gave a sharp nod. "Whatever it takes. It's my fault she was on that ship. I mean to rescue her."

Symphonia cackled. "How very... chivalrous of you." Her gaze darted to Alyana. "And you? Peasant... Lady? Are you part of this venture to rescue the princess?"

Alyana nodded as she stood. She crossed to them, the muscles in her jaw tight. "I am."

"So." Symphonia moved closer still to Derek—he tried not to flinch as her breath hit his skin—and examined him with those yellow eyes. "Will you cover *her* cost as well?"

Alyana's sharp gaze darted to meet his. She tilted her head, a furrow of warning, or concern, in her brow. Her nostrils flared as she opened her mouth.

He held up a hand. "I will. She knows Lady Lydia better than anyone. If we have a chance at bringing her back, I'm sure I'll need her."

Symphonia laughed. Cackled and spun as she clapped her hands. "Two for the princely price of two. Excellent." She tapped her jaw with a pointed nail. "Now... how to go about..." She tutted for a moment before spinning away again and darting to a far shelf.

Derek and Alyana exchanged a glance as the witch lugged a massive caldron to the fire. She chucked it atop the green flames and Derek made to catch it, but it didn't fall. Instead, the thing settled itself gracefully onto the embers of whatever was burning.

"A little of this, a little of that, and what do you know I've made you fat!" Symphonia sang as she gathered armfuls of vials and jars and upended them one at a time into the pot. The liquid within grew, a simmering silver and grey that quickly came to a soft bubble.

The witch paused as she reached for a long and ornate abalone shell box on a topmost shelf. She lowered her hand and glanced at the two of them. "It's a little joke, of course. I'm not making you fat. But you'll have more fat on you. Otherwise, you'd freeze!" She grinned again. She ran a fingernail against the edge of the box and a seal appeared where none had been before.

Flicking it open, Symphonia pulled a tightly coiled scroll from within. "Now." She fixed her gaze on Derek. "Before I put in the final ingredients, a bargain must be struck. Tell me, carefully, *exactly* what you want. Then, I'll tell you the cost."

CHAPTER TEN

Siren or Mermaid

Lydia awoke to a strange sensation. She was floating. Floating and... and alive?

Was she alive?

She inhaled. Her lungs burned as water filled them. There was no choking. No gasp for real breath as the taste of salt found her tongue. Instead, the inhale was slow and painful. An ache that dragged at her body and seemed to pull her downward.

She blinked. Once, twice, a few times until her blurry vision cleared. Her sight was different. Strangely widened. As though her eyes had moved apart. Her peripheral vision showed more than it had before.

She reached hesitant fingers up, touching her cheeks, nose, and finally finding her eyes. The gap between them had widened by over an inch. They sat closer to her temples, giving her an expansive view of the sea around her.

She kept feeling, running her hands down her face and flinching as she reached a set of slits on either side of her neck. Bits of flesh, but hard. Ridged with scales.

Cold hardened into a ball of ice in her stomach. She looked down.

Her dress had ripped, the top of it clung to her shoulders, floating down past her...

A cry erupted from her lips. Below the tattered edges of her dress a tail emerged where her legs should have been. Long. Much longer than she was before, it stretched nearly five feet past her waist, a glittering thing of ivory and cream and pearlescent scales.

Lydia gripped her dress with dark fingers and lifted. The scales crawled up her body, stopping above her hips and bellybutton. They shifted color as they went, the ivory and cream darkening to a shade of black that matched her midnight skin by the time the scales shifted to flesh at her midsection.

Fear took hold then. Terror, as she dropped the dress and spun in a circle, searching. Confusion encompassed her mind as blurred panic told her someone was missing. This was wrong. She remembered her legs. Remembered land.

A ship.

She'd been on a ship. Why though? Who was gone?

She gazed around. There was nothing but water above, sand below, and blue/green darkness on every side.

"He... hello?" Her voice, she recognized her voice. She said it again, surer this time. She was surprised with how similar her voice sounded in these depths as it did on the cliffs.

Cliffs...

Flashes of memory brought her to silence once again. Watching waves crash against rocky shores. Standing on a cliffside, pain radiating through her heart. Pain that pushed her forward. One step at a time closer to the rocks below.

A hand. Fingers wrapping around her wrist, pulling her back.

That pain diminished. The never-ending ache eased by the presence beside her.

She sang. On the cliffs in her memory, and here, now, in the water. Lyrics that came to her tongue as easily as... well, not breathing, but as easily as blinking. A bittersweet love song. Melodic and low.

> *Nothing we know is as true as the sea*
> *Nothing we sing can ease what must be*
> *And though we find hope in each other again*
> *Someday that hope will come to an end...*

Her eyes drifted closed as she sank into this. This thing she could do. This action she understood, craved. A distraction from the confusion, the fear, the desperate search for someone she couldn't remember.

She opened her eyes, and the final note of the song died in her throat. Figures floated before her. They'd have stood taller than men if they had legs. But like her, long tails of shining scales stretched from their midsections down, tapering at the end before flaring out again in vibrant fins.

There were four of them, their eyes set further apart than a human's. Two clutched spears with long fingers, webbed up to the middle knuckle joint. The others carried nothing, though Lydia noted a satchel across one's shoulder and a horn on the other's belt. They all appeared to be female; cloth and seaweed formed wraps around their breasts. Long hair danced with the push and pull of the water, bits of shell, coral, other debris, woven through the strands.

The one with the satchel swam forward. Her sea green tail rippled with the muscles beneath the scales. Her brown hair fluttered behind her.

"Hello, young one," she said, stopping a few feet from where Lydia hovered.

Lydia swallowed. "Hello," she murmured back. "What... what are you?"

A smile showed yellowed, sharpened teeth. "We are mermaids, darling girl. The People of the sea."

A snarl ripped through the water, and Lydia whirled. Nothing at eye level, but as she glanced up, new figures approached.

"Not the only *People* of the sea," came a furious growl.

Lydia scrambled back, digging her hands into the sand beneath her as she tried to figure out how to use her tail to move.

The mermaids had encroached, hovering between her and the new creatures.

They looked much the same. Long tails, scales that glimmered and shone in arrays of color. But these creatures—three of them—wore no coverings above their tails. Their hair was unnaturally smooth, flowing to their waists in beautiful waves. Their hands were long, nails sharp and blackened. Patterns of swirls decorated their skin, different on each, but similar enough to be matching. Their eyes were more forward, more human. They were stunningly beautiful.

The one who'd spoken, a dark creature with red hair and glistening white teeth, had a gnarled scar on her chest, just above her left breast.

"You would stop me greeting her?" she demanded, her gaze fixed on the mermaid with the satchel.

The mermaids were silent, but they held their position in front of Lydia.

Another growl from the creature as she looked past the mermaids and down at Lydia. "There is more than one choice in this sea, child."

Lydia licked her lips, briefly horrified by the sharpness of her teeth, and angled herself into a higher floating position. Her tail took up the effort, moving as naturally as walking as it helped her rise to the height of the others.

"I don't know what you mean."

The one with red hair leaned forward, an eager glint in her eyes. "I knew it. I knew it was you. That voice."

She tilted her head and grinned scornfully at the mermaids before her. "You want her, I assume?"

"She belongs with us," the mermaid with the satchel said in a firm voice.

The other waved her hand, free of webbing, through the water. "She has not decided, look. Look at her hands."

Lydia glanced down. Her hands remained human, no webbing between the fingers.

"Look at her eyes," the mermaid snarled. "Her ship went down. She's ours."

"What..."

They fell silent, gazes on Lydia as she spoke.

"What are *you*?" she directed the question to the newcomers.

The red haired one smiled again. "We're sirens, darling. And you belong with *us*."

CHAPTER ELEVEN

Red as Blood

"We want to get Lydia back." Alyana stepped forward as the sea witch gazed at Derek.

Derek nodded. "We want to find her, and return her to… well, to being human. We want to rescue her from the sea."

Symphonia squinted. "That's it?"

"I suppose…" Derek clicked his teeth, mind rolling over what was going to go wrong here. "We need to bring her back to shore. Not return her to a woman just for her to drown."

Alyana nodded vigorously. "A proper rescue, not a trick."

Symphonia raised an eyebrow. "But that's all. You want to," she waved her hand and rolled her eyes, "*rescue the princess*, but that's it? No perfect marriage, chests of gold, only male heirs, to go with?"

Derek frowned. "No. I just want to get her back. We'll figure out our marriage as we go. As far as gold and males go, my family has more than enough of each. Those don't matter."

"Not to *you*," she grumbled. "I'm happy to help, for the right price. I can't—won't—rescue her for you, but I'll give you the tools to bring her back yourself."

"Both of us," Alyana interjected. "I'll not stay here while he goes after her."

"Wouldn't dream of it, lady." Symphonia showed her sharp toothed grin again. "Now, to the terms of the deal. You'll have three days."

Derek's eyes widened in alarm.

She held up a hand to stop him speaking and continued. "Three days to find her in the sea. Find her and deliver true love's kiss. Then you'll—all of you—be returned to land, legs and all."

Derek briefly wondered what she meant by the legs part, but his focus was stuck on three days. "That doesn't seem enough time... not for the entire sea," he said.

Symphonia slide her free hand up to her neck and gripped a chord of leather. She revealed a seashell that had been hidden beneath her dress. "This will guide you."

She pulled it over her head, careful with her crown, and handed it to Derek. He glanced at Alyana. She gave a brief nod, and he slipped it over his head.

The weight of it surprised him. The shell was thin, but the chord was heavy against his neck.

"Now," Symphonia waved the scroll in her hand in his face, "on to my payment. I'll do this for you..." Her yellow eyes glinted. "In exchange for your kingdom."

Derek's mouth went dry as a pang shot through his chest. "Not on your life," he said in an exhale.

"That was fast. Interesting..." Symphonia showed her teeth. "You're sure? You don't want the deal?"

"Hold on." Alyana held up a hand, her voice desperate. She strode to Derek and faced him head on. Close enough that he could feel her breath on his throat; she glared up at him and hissed, "What are you doing? We *have* to get Lydia back. If this is what it takes, so be it."

Derek's expression shifted. His wide eyes narrowed, brow furrowing as he glared at her. "Give us a moment?" His gaze darted to the witch as he asked.

She nodded, one eyebrow raised in a slightly amused expression.

Derek gestured for Alyana to take a few paces away to give them some privacy. She obliged, still watching him.

"I have a responsibility to this land," Derek said in a low voice. "This kingdom, and the people in it, are under my protection. I will not trade that trust, that sanctity, for anything."

Alyana took a few angry breaths, nostrils flaring. "What of Lydia?"

Derek swallowed and ran a hand across his forehead. "I'll think of something. A trade usually involves bargaining, doesn't it?"

Alyana bit her lip. After a few seconds she nodded.

Derek turned back to Symphonia. "What else do you want? I won't risk my kingdom or its future."

She surprised him with a fanged grin. "All part of the fun, prince. Figuring out what her life is worth to you."

Derek glanced to Alyana at that. Noted the tears gleaming in her eyes, her knuckles white as she clenched her hands into fists. She stepped forward. He put his hand up, but she ignored it.

"I have little to give," Alyana murmured.

Symphonia's stare darted to the redheaded woman. Her eyes widened, gleaming. "Indeed. Little to give, much to lose."

"But," Alyana pressed on, "name your price to me and I shall pay it. Please."

Symphonia approached, scroll still in hand, and tilted her head at Alyana. "You'd pay anything?"

Alyana nodded.

The witch reached up with her free hand. Her fingers went to Alyana's throat, slow enough that Derek didn't draw his sword, but he stepped forward, ready.

Alyana held still; the only movement came from her shallow breathing as Symphonia gently traced her throat with the pads of her fingers.

After a moment the witch shook her head. "Not that..."
Alyana sniffed.

"Give me a moment, lady. Perhaps you have something that might lower the price for the prince."

Her fingers moved up Alyana's chin and jaw, untucking a strand of her vibrant red hair. Symphonia curled it around her fingers.

"This."

"What?" Alyana glanced at her, confusion rather than fear in her eyes.

"This. Red as blood, bright as day. It will look pretty with my other things." She gestured at the shelves of objects. "Besides." Her head tilted again. "Hair like this is a good ingredient."

Derek swallowed a grunt at the thought of someone eating hair. Then he realized she probably meant potions or the like. Then his gut twisted at the notion that she might mean both things.

"Yes, yes of course." Alyana drew her dagger, grabbed her braid, and made to cut.

"*Wait!*" Symphonia held up a hand, alarmed. "Hold a moment, silly girl. Let us finish the deal before you ruin it. Besides, I need to be the one to cut it."

Alyana froze, hands trembling, and then lowered the blade to her side. "Right." She looked at Derek. "Highness?"

CHAPTER TWELVE

A Library of Bad Decisions

Derek exhaled. He ran a hand through his blonde hair as both the handmaiden and the witch turned to look at him. "I can't," he muttered. "I can't give you my kingdom."

Symphonia scrunched up her nose. "We established that part, prince. The question now is, what *can* you give me?"

Derek put out his hands, rather feebly. "What else do you want? I'm a crown prince. I can get you jewels, gems." He gave an exasperated sigh. "The red hair from every citizen in the land."

The witch snorted. "Gems and jewels from the land have no value when compared to the treasures of the sea. As for the hair," she gestured to Alyana, "that should be enough to last me a few decades."

Derek blinked, a brief curiosity of her age flitting into his mind before he focused back on the task at hand. "Very well, what ingredients do you require, or desire, that *are* difficult for you to obtain?"

"Hmm." She stared at a far corner of the cavern, eyes dimming for a moment as she scratched her chin. Her fingernail tapped against one of the black cracks snaking across her skin. "That is a unique offer. There are fungi from the dark mountain caves. Flowers only grown in the north. Many things." She returned her focus to him. "Many things I could use, were I able to reach them."

Derek nodded, hope flaring in his chest. "Name them, I'll have people collect everything you need."

She squinted, irritation in her gaze. With a heavy sigh, she rolled her eyes at Alyana. "*Royalty.*"

Alyana opened her mouth, then shut it again and simply nodded.

"Prince, I cannot have *other* people touching my things. *Delicate.* These are delicate ingredients. And delicate processes are required for collecting them."

"What can I do then?" Derek demanded, heat rising in his cheeks. This back and forth was feeling more and more impossible.

"Release me, of course." Symphonia scurried up to him, and he took a startled step back. Her yellow gaze bored into him. "Grant me the freedom to explore the kingdom you love so much."

"Are you not able to do so now?" Alyana stepped forward, eyebrows drawn together in a frown.

"No," Symphonia hissed, a flash of anger striking across her expression. She gestured at him with the scroll still coiled in her grasp. "The prince's great-great grandparents made their own deal, ages ago. I'm afraid I got the short end on that one."

Derek fell half a step back, his chest tightening. He opened his mouth, but no words came out.

"You're trapped here?" Alyana murmured.

"Not quite. Deals are tricky," Symphonia said. "I cannot set foot on the kingdom proper as long as his," she gestured at Derek, "bloodline rules. I have plenty of other places to go. But this land..." Her lip curled into a snarl. "This land was *my* home before the cities were formed. Before the crown was molded." She blinked and the ferocity in her gaze eased. "It has changed much. I wish to see it."

"What did you..." Derek swallowed. There was no way to ask the question tactfully, so he went for straightforward. "Why did they banish you from the kingdom?"

Symphonia raised an eyebrow. "I didn't say they banished me." She turned and walked back to the shelf, setting the scroll down. "A deal has three parts. What you want. What I want. And the consequence. The situation with your grandparents resulted in a consequence on my end. One that has kept me from your lands for a long time."

Derek remained silent, waiting for her to continue. To explain.

"You want to get the princess. I want to go back onto land. Then, we each chose a consequence. The thing that happens when one of us fails or breaks the bargain. To keep..." She exhaled, her focus going distant for a moment. "To keep us honest."

"What is the consequence this time?" Alyana murmured.

"Well." Symphonia's eyes regained their focus and she grinned at Alyana. "I was hoping it would be the kingdom. But since that doesn't seem to be in the cards..." She stared at Derek, flickering light from the green fire reflecting in her eyes. "Something simpler. Something that won't cause any danger to your people."

He nodded.

"Your title."

Confusion swept him. He frowned, tilting his head. "What do you mean?"

"Your position as crown prince. No harm will come to you, or your family, but if you fail... if you *break* this bargain... you forfeit your crown."

Derek opened and closed his mouth like a fish hauled onto a dock. His tongue went dry as he struggled for words.

"His family," Alyana said, stepping closer, "they'd still hold the throne?"

Symphonia rolled her eyes, but then she nodded. "The notion of any monarchy is outdated and boring. But yes. His bloodline will hold the throne."

Alyana turned to Derek. He grimaced against the pleading in her eyes.

"We *have* to do this. You *have* to do this. It's our only way to get her back."

Derek ran a hand across his jaw. He looked to Symphonia. "You promise no one in my family, or the kingdom, will be harmed?"

"Not by me," Symphonia sang.

Derek glowered. A growl of frustration sounded in his throat.

"Oh hush," she snapped. "They will not be harmed by any making of this bargain. The deal between us will have no effect on their wellbeing. That said, you're talking about an entire kingdom. I'm not about to promise none of them will be harmed while you're finding the princess."

He pursed his lips, breath uneven.

"They will not be harmed by *me*," the witch clarified.

Derek mulled it over in his mind. He tried to find a catch. A break in her words that might render everything they'd discussed useless. He tried to find a hole in *his* words, a way to keep his great great-grandparent's bargain intact.

A full minute passed while he stood lost in thought. Eventually, Alyana put a hand on his arm.

"Derek."

He jerked. His blue eyes met her green ones. Her face was hard with determination.

"It's a good deal. We have to take it."

"What will your consequence be?" Derek asked, turning once again to the witch.

She shrugged. "What would you choose?"

He clenched his jaw, mind racing as fast as his heartbeat. "No more deals."

An audible exhale left Symphonia's lips. She stared at him.

"No bargains, not ever again."

She shook her head, slowly. "I can't agree to that. *Never* again? Do you know how long witches live without deals? Trades?"

"A year."

They both looked at Alyana.

She said it again, glancing from one to the other. "If the bargain is broken. The deal forfeited... You don't make bargains for a year, and you lose your crown."

Derek bit his cheek. "And if we succeed..."

"Then none of it matters. You get the princess; I get to explore the kingdom. It's done. No consequence." Symphonia reached for the scroll again. As her fingers touched the paper, scrawling letters of gold appeared.

A chill went down Derek's spine at the sight. At the weight of it. At the realization of what he was about to do.

"Decide now, prince." Symphonia unrolled the scroll. "I have all the time in the world, but my patience is running thin."

He moved forward to look. The words, written in the common tongue and easily read, showed no deception. No hint at an underlying scheme.

Still... his mother's warnings echoed in his ears.

He reached out a hand. She gave him a quill from a jar on a shelf.

"No ink is necessary. You're binding this with your soul, not just your name."

He swallowed. He signed his name.

The scroll furled itself up, pulling from his hands, and—on its own accord—settled itself on the shelf with the others. All stacked together like a little library of bad decisions.

"Wonderful," Symphonia sang. "Three days." Her grin widened an unnatural amount. "Three days to rescue a princess from the depths of the sea."

Alyana sucked in a breath. Derek held his.

Symphonia slapped her hands together. "Let's get to it. I have a potion to finish."

CHAPTER THIRTEEN

Tails of the Deep

Derek plugged his nose as Symphonia tilted his head back with one hand. Her nails dug into the base of his neck as she poured a thin stream of golden liquid into his mouth. The taste wasn't as bad as he expected, not with all he'd watched her pour into that cauldron.

Alyana went next. Her hair was tied back into a much thinner braid than before. Symphonia had shaved her head from the base to a little above her ears. She gulped down the potion with no complaint.

"A few warnings," Symphonia said quietly as the two of them stared at her. "You'll have trouble breathing at first. Do not panic. Water does not feel the same as air."

Derek swallowed but nodded.

"There are many dangers in the sea," she continued. "Many which you're familiar with, sharks, pirates, fishermen, and the like. There are also many you don't know about. Keep wary. Do not let down your guard."

Alyana gripped the hilt of the small dagger at her side.

"Your princess," Symphonia looked from Derek to Alyana and back, "has been in the water for days. She might not be the way you remember. She may be... changed. Her memory..." A dark shadow flickered across the witch's face. "Dying plays tricks on the mind and the heart. Be careful when you approach her."

Anxiety swam through Derek's gut, along with a churning sensation that had nothing to do with his thoughts about Lydia. His skin itched. His pants were too tight at the top. He'd already discarded his boots and was grateful he did so as his feet began to tingle.

"Lastly..." Symphonia walked around the two of them, her toes dipping into the water before them.

They stood at the mouth of the cave, inches from the waves lapping onto the rock. The urge to go forward surged within Derek's chest. He bit his lip and held firm, listening.

"This," Symphonia pressed her fingers against the heavy shell resting on his chest, "is no mere trinket. It is a marker that will lead you to the princess."

He nodded.

"It is also precious to me. A sign of our barter. Should you lose it, or break it, our deal ends. Do you understand?"

Derek's focus flickered. His gaze caught on the numerous shells and pale white fragments of the witch's crown. The sight of it in the sunlight was so different from the green flames within her cavern. She looked smaller here.

Less a terrifying creature from his mother's stories and more like a person, fragile as the cracks on her face.

"Do you understand, prince?" she demanded.

Alyana reached out and gripped Derek's hand. He shook himself and nodded.

"I understand."

"Well then." Symphonia circled around the two of them. Her hand rested on Derek's back. "You'd better get to it. Three days," she glanced at the sun, "starting now."

Without warning, she shoved. Derek fell forward into the water, catching himself on the sand a few inches below the surface. Alyana did the same, the end of her braid dripping into the salty liquid.

Again, that urge filled Derek's chest. The urge to go under, to let every inch of his skin be exposed to the cool water. He glanced back at the sea witch.

She gave the smallest wave, lips widened into a sharp-toothed grin, and disappeared back into her home.

His gaze followed her out of sight, and then it caught on something else. Something that filled him both with terror and excitement. His feet were no longer feet.

His pants, torn to shreds, hung from the edges of a shimmering blue and gold tail. Several feet longer than his already long legs, it stretched behind him and flapped against the rock. It wanted to be under. *He* wanted to be under.

"So." He looked to Alyana, who was staring wide eyed at her own tail. "Shall we save a princess?"

The hint of a grin flickered across her face. Without a word, she dug her hands into the sand, pulled herself into deeper water, and dove beneath the waves.

Chapter Fourteen

Unfinished Business

Lydia's head swam. Four mermaids floated before her, blocking the sirens from her path. She glanced at her hands again. They did look like other sirens', but there was something else...

She touched a silver band on her left ring finger. It was simple, a flower-like cluster of miniscule diamonds across the top with sapphires sprouting from it like leaves. She didn't recognize it.

She didn't recognize many things beyond her own voice. But this... a frown creased her brow as the beings ahead continued to discuss who she belonged to. The conversation sounded familiar. Certain words caught hold of her. Drove bitter blades through her chest and gut. *Ours, belong, not your decision.*

She closed her eyes and blocked out the myriad of voices. Instead, she focused again on the ring. On the feeling that came with it. A feeling of a task yet to be done. A purpose needing to be filled.

There was something...

"There's something I'm supposed to do," Lydia murmured.

The conversation ahead of her stopped. The mermaids with their widened eyes and sharp teeth, turned to look at her. The sirens, with their flowing hair and human features, took the opportunity to swim forward. The two groups now formed a half-circle around her.

"What do you mean?" The siren, the one with red hair and dark skin and scales darted past the mermaid at this. Her hand went out, reaching for Lydia as the mermaids behind her snarled.

"I..." Lydia swallowed. "I have something I have to do."

A smile split the thick, lush lips of the siren before her. The hand, with those blackened fingernails curved to points, rested on her shoulder. The siren nodded. "You have unfinished business."

"I... Yes," Lydia said, staring up at her.

"*No*," the mermaid snapped.

The siren turned; triumph flushed across her cheeks. She hooked her arm under Lydia's and pulled her along past the throng of mermaids. "You heard the girl," she said with a snide grin. "She has unfinished business. That's *our* business."

Lydia floated along with the pull of the siren's arm, confusion muddling her mind. This situation, this argument between two underwater creatures, it was so unimportant compared to the roiling worry in her heart and mind.

Someone was missing. Someone who was on the same ship she was. She was sure of it.

Her gaze drifted to the ring on her finger.

"Listen."

A grip on her arm, tighter than the siren's, drew her back to the present. She met the gaze of the green tailed mermaid. The wide eyes were unsettling, but not far enough apart to make meeting them impossible.

"They aren't what you want to be. You seem like a good person. A kind person. The songs you sing could be used for good. For helping people. Don't let these..." She snarled, sharp pointed teeth pulling an exhale of fear from Lydia's lips. "Creatures... use you to hurt people."

Her words were so jarring, so different from the glint of fury in her eyes and the inhuman qualities of her face, that Lydia didn't know what to make of it. She drifted, confused, and scared, and barely able to talk let alone chose...

"We will watch," the mermaid said. Her bright gaze flicked to the siren then back to Lydia. "We will watch and wait and if you change your mind... we will be there."

The siren pulled her along, past the mermaids, and deeper into the dark water. The other two of her kind caressed Lydia's shoulders and back with their soft human hands as they moved away.

"It's all right, sister. You're with us now. We will keep you safe. Protect you. And when the time comes, we will complete our unfinished business together."

Lydia nodded. She barely had to turn her head to see the mermaids, unmoving apart from the gentle swish of their tails. They watched, disappearing into the dark, as she and the sirens swam away.

CHAPTER FIFTEEN

Under the Sea

"This is amazing."

The awe in Alyana's voice brought a grin to Derek's lips. She was right. It was amazing.

They swam close enough to see each other, far enough apart to get used to the strength and length of their new tails. Sea life moved past them, seemingly unaffected by their presence. Turtles, massive things with multicolored shells, schools of silver and gold fish, eels, and so much more he didn't have names for.

They swam over a bed of coral, and Derek nearly ran into a cluster of seaweed he was so distracted by the sight.

He looked up just in time, jerked to the side, rolled, and kept rolling a few times before he figured out which way to flick his tail to stop it. As he righted himself, Alyana cackled a few feet away, one hand over her mouth, not quite stifling the sound.

She'd tied the ends of her dress in a loop where her scales met her skin. Her tail was as red as her hair, with streaks of dark shimmering green running throughout the scales.

Derek gave her a squinty-eyed glare but couldn't help a chuckle as he sucked in a chest-full of water. It was a strange thing. Well, all of it was strange. But breathing water might have been the strangest for him. It was heavy, thick. Like running on a day so full of fog you couldn't see a foot ahead of you, but multiplied a thousand times.

"Your..." Alyana stopped cackling and swam forward. She reached up a hand, her pale fingers going toward his face before she stopped herself. "Your eyes are... different."

"What?" Derek asked, alarmed. He blinked. Blinked again. A realization crept into his mind that he shouldn't be able to see all the things he could see. He put tentative fingers to his face and gasped at the distance between his eyes. He looked at Alyana. "Why aren't yours like this?" he demanded.

She shrugged a freckled shoulder. "Our tails are the same. Maybe my eyes will change as we go?"

He nodded, a wary shiver going through his chest. He pushed through the water barely using his arms; the power of his tail was more than enough to propel him forward.

The witch hadn't lied when she'd said they needed to have a little more fat. His tail was thick, muscles oddly familiar to use. He gazed at it for a moment. His skin melted into scales just below his ribcage, an array of blue with hints of gold. He enjoyed the rippling effect as the barest hints of sunlight made their way through the depths to glint off his tail.

"Which way?" Alyana asked for the fifth time.

Derek's hand rose to the shell around his neck, lighter in the water, but still secure against his chest. He lifted it. Let it float for a brief moment before it moved. A gentle tug on the chord securing it to him as the thing pulled in a slightly left direction. He pointed.

Alyana gave a nod, and the two continued on.

"Why did you bring that?" she asked after a few minutes of silence. They'd passed the coral, and as they swam further from the shore fewer and fewer creatures crossed their path.

He followed her eyeline to the belt around his waist. His sword was still attached to the leather, sheathed at his side.

"Why not?" he said with a raised eyebrow. He'd lost his pants when they dove into the water. They'd been shredded to bits anyway. So far he'd kept his mind distracted from such thoughts as relieving himself, or what he'd be wearing—not wearing—when they were transported back to land.

"We're in salt water, Derek. It's going to rust in the scabbard."

He glared at her. "I'd rather have it than not. You heard the witch. There are dangers out here. Besides." He raised an eyebrow. "You brought that little dagger."

She scoffed. "I don't imagine my little dagger is worth as much as your sword."

He shrugged, the motion accidently sending him sideways. He corrected course and nodded. "Getting a new sword won't be a problem."

"Right, crown prince and all," she said. "You can get anything you want."

He let out a bitter laugh. "To a limit."

"All things have a limit. Yours happens to be immeasurably higher than most."

He frowned at her tone. The bitterness laced in her words. "Listen, I didn't choose to be born a prince. Let alone the eldest." He heaved a sigh, wanting to continue but fully aware that any attempt at complaint would have him coming across like the spoiled rich boy he—arguably—was.

Alyana shrugged a shoulder and careened right into him.

"Oomph, sorry," she groaned as she swerved away.

"Shrugging," he laughed, "who knew. Maybe this is one of the dangers of the sea Symphonia was talking about."

Alyana rolled her eyes. "Have you thought about what we're going to eat down here?"

"Honestly, I'm hoping we find Lydia before I get hungry. Anything beyond that I'm trying not to think about."

Her high laugh filled the water around them. "Me too. I suppose if we wait until we're hungry enough, we will find something we won't mind eating raw."

Derek winced. "So much for not thinking about it."

She laughed again.

They swam a little longer before he stopped to check their heading once again. A nagging flicker of doubt warned that trusting the witch's shell might not be the best way to find Lydia. Still, with the consequences in place for both of them… she wouldn't purposefully lead them astray. Would she?

The doubt grew as they swam further out to sea.

"How did you meet? How did a servant and a princess become such close friends?" he asked after a long bout of silence.

Alyana glanced at him, green eyes wide, though physically still in the normal place on her face. She hesitated a moment, then swallowed. "She saved my life, and I hers."

CHAPTER SIXTEEN

We Cannot Fail

"I was fourteen," Alyana said. Her voice was low, the teasing tone gone as she and Derek swam side-by-side. The shell continued to pull them away from land and, as they got further out to sea, it started taking them deeper as well.

"My parents were simple folk. We lived just outside the capital. Farmers, tending crops on land we didn't own and had no control over."

Derek nodded. The practice wasn't unheard of for most Lords. They let peasants live on their acreage in exchange for them working the fields and cattle. His mother had been instituting different policies across the kingdom before she'd fallen ill. Most of the land utilized by farmers was now owned by them in some way shape of form. Most, but not all. Not yet.

"We had just enough," she continued. "Never anything extra, but always enough to feed me and my brothers. Four of them." She swallowed. "My fourteenth year saw an infected crop followed by a hard winter. I was the only thing worth any money in our home, so my parents decided the best way to keep the family going was to sell me off."

A weight that had nothing to do with the shell settled heavy and tight against Derek's chest.

"There were a few wealthier families we knew from the city. A cobbler my father bought shoes from. A baker whose wife my mother was friendly with. A couple of others. Some had sons. Some were men older than my father in need of a wife." Her voice shook, tremors of fury audible in her exhales.

Derek said nothing.

"They dressed me up, pinched my cheeks red, and put handfuls of ridiculous flowers in my hair. Everyone who saw us on the road knew what we were doing. They knew I wouldn't return." She fell silent for a few minutes.

"I'm…" Derek glanced at her, and though the sea disguised it, the red of her eyes told him if they'd been on land, he'd have seen tears. "I'm sorry, Alyana."

She shook her head. "The Viscount and Viscountess were out that day. In the city, shopping for their daughter. It was a whole commotion. Guards everywhere, searches through every gate." She paused. A bitter smile split her lips. "I ran. I offered to be searched first, at the farthest gate we planned to go through, about halfway into the city toward the palace. When the guard moved onto my mother, I hiked up my skirt and took off."

The smile widened. Derek slowed, and Alyana mimicked him. She faced him, flicking her tail side to side.

"I was always the fastest, and it's not like the guards cared enough to help track down a farm girl. They'd dressed me up, so I got through another two gates before the city guard wouldn't let me further." She gripped the tail of her braid, still long enough to dangle past her shoulders. "It was far enough. Lydia saw me. She was stuck in a stupid carriage while her parents went shop to shop picking things out for her. She saw me panic at the gate and called me to her. I don't know what it was... beyond foolish." She shook her head. "But something about her voice drew me in. Told me it'd be all right."

He nodded, studying her face. The anger was still there. Rage glinting in her eyes, hands clenched into fists. But as she spoke of Lydia, the furrow in her brow smoothed. Her lips curved into a smile.

"She brought me in then. Demanded to make me her handmaiden. Even with my peasant's voice and the dirt on my hem. The Viscount was ready to toss me in a cell for even getting into the carriage, but Lydia's mother stopped him. They gave me a chance."

She met his eye, her hands clenched into fists for a brief moment. "I took it. And I never looked back."

Derek fiddled with his belt for a few seconds. "I'm... I truly am sorry for what your family tried to do. That sort of thing..." He grimaced. "I'm sure it happens, but it's heavily frowned upon in our kingdom."

She scoffed. "Tell that to the boxes of gems and gold we carried on the ship."

He nodded, gut churning. "I can't deny, being paraded before the court feels something like being livestock at market. Still..."

He couldn't continue because there was nothing else to say. No words to make it better. Nothing to negate the fact that he and Lady Lydia had essentially been sold to each other by their families. The thought drove away any hunger he felt with a wave of nausea.

Alyana brushed a hand down her braid, twirling the end between her fingers. "She saved me, Derek. She saved me, and she's been my closest friend ever since. I can't let her down in this. We cannot fail."

CHAPTER SEVENTEEN

Freedom in the Stars

The sea around them changed as evening fell. The water, comfortable up until that point, grew cold. Derek had been surprised by how much he could see in the deep, but even with his altered vision it soon became too dark to make out more than a few yards ahead.

"We should stop."

Alyana, a bit ahead, came to a halt. The two had gotten used to the movements of their tails, bodies, and how it all connected.

It was draining, exhausting to swim for hours on end. Derek's abs burned, the new muscles under his scales aching as he hovered in the water, watching Alyana. She wouldn't want to stop; he knew it. But they had to rest.

"Why?" she demanded.

Derek shook his head and ran a hand through his hair. "It's getting cold, my tail hurts, and we want to have our strength tomorrow."

"We have no idea how close we are. What if she's still days away?"

Derek sighed and angled upward. The surface was far, far above. He swam toward it.

Alyana grunted her disapproval but followed.

Derek hesitated as glimmering light came into view. Moonlight poured down, sending shafts of silver through the water. He glanced at his companion. "I'll take a look at the stars, see how far we are from where the ship sank."

"All right then. If we're still far, I want to keep going."

Derek nodded. "That sounds fair."

He swam up. It felt wrong when his head broke the surface. He inhaled, but the air collided with the water already in his lungs and he couldn't gulp down a breath. He choked. Coughed. Water poured from his lips.

When there was room for air... it burned. Burned and scalded and hurt. He exhaled, dipped back beneath the surface, and sucked in a cooling chest-full of water.

"That was quick." Alyana raised an eyebrow.

Derek rubbed his chest with his palm, grimacing. "I can't breathe."

"What?" She swam forward, concern replacing incredulity.

"Up there." He pointed, a shiver running down his spine. "I can't breathe air anymore."

Alarm flickered across her face. "It's fine. It will go back to normal after we find Lydia and you... you and she..."

Heat rushed to Derek's cheeks. He nodded. "Right."

"Until then, can't you just hold your breath?"

"Ah." Derek flushed even more. "Yes, that does seem a logical solution." He inhaled and, holding the water in, popped his head back above the surface.

The sky was alight, the moon full and huge at the edge of the distant horizon. Stars twinkled above him. Their light reflected across the gently lapping surface of the sea. The wind was soft, a breeze that chilled his hair but left the water relatively undisturbed.

The peace down below was dark and tight. It was different. A kind of freedom he couldn't help enjoying, even though the pressure of their task was still at the forefront of his mind.

This though... this view of the sea...

It was one thing to be on a ship, destination set, royal guards close at hand. It was another thing entirely to watch the stars from where he was now.

He ducked back down, let out the water in his lungs, and took in a new batch. Alyana crossed her arms.

"You should come look at this," he murmured.

"You should hurry up," she said.

He bobbed his head and went back up. This time he focused on the stars, on their placement in the sky. He paddled the water with his hands, twisting this way and that to figure out their position. A moment later he dove back down.

"We're close. Close enough that we might even find the ship if we went to the bottom."

"You're thinking of taking shelter there through the night?"

He nodded. "I don't know about you, but this has made me a lot hungrier than riding."

"I don't want to eat raw fish," she groaned.

Derek laughed, and the two of them flipped and dove, their powerful tails propelling them down. His hunger grew as they moved deeper. The cold pressed against him from all sides, the dark eventually slowing their pace to a crawl.

"There..." Alyana's voice startled him after their long silence.

His gaze followed where her finger pointed. Just ahead of them, looming out of the dark, was the wreckage of the ship they'd been on only days ago.

"Were there..." Alyana swallowed. She glanced at him, shadows of something dark in her gaze. "Were there other women on the ship? Besides Lydia and me?"

Derek shook his head. "Only Ruth."

Alyana let out a breath through her lips. "Well then, where too?"

Derek rubbed his hands together. "I think the kitchen is a good place to start. I'm not keen on fishing at the moment..." He glanced at his tail with a grimace.

"Will there be anything still good?" Alyana asked with a raised eyebrow.

Derek let out a low chuckle. "I imagine the bread has gone soggy, but there has to be *something* we can find."

They swam close together, hands occasionally brushing, tails doing the same, as they made their way through the wreckage. The portion of the ship they'd come across was only half. Derek was sure if they searched the area, they'd find the rest. The hull had split with the force of the waves. Entering was not a difficult thing.

"I wish I could see like this on land," Derek murmured after a few careful minutes. They'd reached the long hallway on the second level. Even here, completely obscured from any light source, he was still able to make out the shapes around them. The rough wooden walls and floor—everything slanted now the ship lay on its side—doors leading to private rooms, crew quarters, storage compartments; he'd recognize the kitchen when they came to it.

"You'd have trouble in the light," Alyana said, her voice equally low. "It would hurt your eyes, maybe even damage them. Besides," he caught a glimpse of her grin, "I doubt the ladies would be as interested with your eyes like that, prince or not."

Her tone brought a chuckle rather than annoyance.

"Fair point. Still, being able to see in the dark like this—"

He stopped, heart hammering against his chest. Alyana gasped. Her fingers clenched around his arm. He put his hand atop hers. He swallowed, grief rising in his stomach.

Just ahead of them, where the stairs led to the deck, floated the corpse of the captain.

Mother's Mourn

"Should have expected this, I suppose," Derek muttered. He clenched his jaw, fighting the trembling of his lips and the tears in his eyes.

Alyana squeezed his arm. "Is there another way around?"

Derek shook his head. "We don't have to go past. The kitchen is there." He gestured above where the door closest to the stairs stood ajar. The ship wasn't entirely sideways, but enough that they'd have to swim up to get in.

Alyana nodded.

Derek didn't move. His gaze was fixed on the body of the captain. Bloated and lifeless, the gentle current around them causing it to bump against the stairs. Behind it—him—the opening leading to the deck was a pit of black.

They hadn't known each other well. Derek's only time on this particular ship had been his voyage to collect Lydia and the few days they'd had on the return trip. Charles knew him. Charles had been on the ship a dozen times over the past few years. Their father didn't mind the second son venturing out to sea.

Charles had spoken fondly of the captain.

"I don't know..." Alyana hesitated, only continuing after Derek wrenched his gaze from the body and met her eye. "We burn ours. I don't know if you'd want to try to bury him or..."

Derek shook his head. "There wouldn't be much use for that down here. Besides, if he'd died on land he'd have wanted to be pushed out to sea." He swallowed. "This isn't how it should have gone, but he'd be grateful to be with his ship."

He blinked against the burning in his eyes, took Alyana's hand, and led her through the door to the kitchen.

The bread they found was indeed a soggy pile of mush. Small silver fish, barely the size of Derek's pinky finger, were feasting on the meal.

Derek swallowed his nausea, glad they'd found the fish eating bread instead of the other options in the sunken wreckage. After opening a few barrels and digging through cabinets, they found porridge, fully soaked but edible. Derek uncovered a fair amount of jerky that had been sealed well enough that no fish had gotten to it. They also found a box of tea, but with no way to contain it they left it where it was.

"I thought it'd be saltier," Alyana said with a mouthful of food.

They'd nestled against a wall away from the door. The porthole looked down onto the sandy seabed. Derek's tail did not enjoy pressing against the wood, but he had no desire to keep moving any of his muscles. He'd removed his belt and sword, looping one end around his wrist to keep them floating away.

Derek nodded, a bite of bland porridge swishing in his mouth. He swallowed. "I don't taste it anymore, the salt. Maybe because we're breathing the water. It still feels thick in my chest, but it isn't drying me out like I worried it might. It's odd, not needing to drink."

They ate their fill. Derek, still cold, gathered a tarp to drape over them. It didn't help much, but the sensation of covers eased his mind somewhat.

"I don't think I'll be able to sleep," Alyana muttered.

They sat shoulder to shoulder against what had been the floor, their tails sticking out the end of the tarp. It wasn't comfortable exactly, but with a full belly and not having to tense against the current, it was enough to relax.

Derek jerked his head up. He'd been seconds away from sleep, dozing in the gentle push and pull. He leaned back again, eyes drifting closed.

"Want me to close the door?" he offered, his voice slurred with exhaustion.

"It's not that," she said. "I can't stop thinking about Lydia."

He opened his eyes.

"What if *she's* hungry? What if she's cold and alone and scared? There was no one there to explain. She didn't have a sea witch to warn her of the dangers. What if she's too far gone?" She sniffed. "What if she doesn't remember me?"

Derek swallowed the rising anxiety in his chest. He moved his arm, lifting it from the warmth of the tarp and taking her hand. She glanced at him as his fingers encompassed hers.

"What ifs won't help," he said. "Lydia won't forget you. She saved you, right? You two are by each other's side, no matter what."

"And if she's a siren?" Alyana whispered, her voice choked on tears.

"I wanted to ask about that." Derek angled sideways to see her more clearly. He was fully awake now, sleep driven from him like they'd driven the fish from the cupboards. "Symphonia explained a little, but I'm still not clear on the difference between a siren and a mermaid."

Alyana's hand trembled in his. "Your Old Tales say a woman who dies at sea becomes a mermaid. Our stories have a darker current. Most women who die at sea are not victims of storms. They're victims of men. Sailors who grew paranoid and threw them over. Jealous lovers... angry fathers... It wasn't uncommon, not so long ago, for unmarried women of a certain age to be tossed onto a ship for company on the voyage only to be killed before they reached their destination."

Derek's grip on her hand tightened for a brief moment before he let her go, both hands clenched into fists in his lap. "Those practices, they're still allowed in your kingdom?"

"Not allowed. Not anymore. But the sea is still a treacherous place for a woman."

Derek nodded. "The ones who are murdered... they become sirens."

"So say our stories. They aren't the only ones. There's a..." She hesitated. Her fingers fiddled with a hole in the tarp. "There's a set of cliffs not far from the palace. They call it Mother's Mourn. It's where some women go when there's no hope. When they have nothing left to live for."

Derek's blood went cold. "They... they jump?"

She nodded. "Those ones become sirens too. That pain... the fear or fury or despair that drives them off the edge, it's part of the transformation."

"How do you know all of this?" he asked, his voice soft.

She met his gaze. Her lips trembled as she pressed them together, tight enough that they went white. She swallowed.

"Oh," Derek whispered. "That's where you saved *her* life... you..." His brow furrowed, sadness filling him. "You stopped her from jumping."

Alyana nodded again. "It was a few years ago. Her uncle, the king, he wanted to marry her off to a warlord from an empire in distant lands. The voyage itself would have taken months. And the man..." She grimaced, a flash of fury lighting through her green eyes. "He was a cruel, disgusting thing."

Derek nodded. "I know the empire you speak of. We've had our own dealings with them, none pleasant." He frowned. "But Lydia and I have been engaged since we were ten. How would..."

"That's what stopped it," Alyana muttered. "The Viscountess reminded the king that Lydia was already spoken for, and by an ally much closer and arguably more powerful than the empire. But it took weeks. Weeks and weeks of arguments and discussions. None of the which included Lydia. She managed to slip away during a particularly intense shouting match, and I followed."

"How old—"

"If they'd gone through with breaking your engagement, she'd have been sixteen by the time they married."

They fell into silence for a few long minutes. Derek felt an odd stirring of gratitude for his father's insistence that none of his children marry before their eighteenth birthday. His sisters had received handfuls of suitors, constantly vying for his father's attention and interest. A few had stoked it, but each had been warned that the girls wouldn't be wed until they were of age.

"What would it mean," he finally asked, "if she were a siren instead of a mermaid?"

"According to our stories, it would mean that instead of living at the bottom of the sea with other mermaids in their own sort of society, she'd stay near the surface. She'd cling to rocks and sing to sailors. She'd draw ships toward dangerous reefs, wait for them to run aground or wreck, and then she'd feed on the bodies of the men on those ships."

CHAPTER NINETEEN

Not Unhappy

Lydia's eyes shifted. Through the night whatever magic had given her wider sight had seen fit to return her features to the more human-like ones the sirens enjoyed. She'd slept in their home, a massive cavern system in the rocky cliff-side of some coast or another. Her teeth had stopped their unnatural sharp growth but had yet to return to normal. Her fingers had slight webbing between the knuckles.

Her memories hadn't returned with her features. The only clues she had from her life before drowning were the ring on her finger and the heavy weight on her heart. She caught herself glancing around every few minutes, searching for the missing presence. It was like a piece of her had been carved away when the ship went down.

The only moments when the aching loss dimmed were when the sirens invited her to sing.

Lucia, the one with bright red hair and soft amber skin, had ensured the others give Lydia space. She'd showed her to a small room. The sirens slept on hammocks rather than beds. Lydia's was a ragged thing of stained sail, but it kept her comfortable. It let her relax the long tail she was still getting used to.

The days passed with something that couldn't be called ease, but Lydia wasn't *unhappy*. She ate the food they served, different braids of seaweed, raw prepared fish, and a collection of shelled things they used little driftwood carved forks to pry out. She sang with them in the caverns, enjoying the collection of voices. She taught them her song and learned theirs. She traced patterns with the glowing mossy seaweed they used to lighten their home.

"Are you going out again?" she asked Lucia during breakfast on her fourth day.

The sunrise and set had been invisible to her since she'd drowned. The sirens didn't say they were keeping her in their home, but they seemed relieved when she showed little curiosity to explore.

Each day at dawn the women gathered at the entrance to their caves. Lydia had watched them go, craving solitude for a few hours, and too nervous to ask where they were going. Today however, her itch to do something, to stretch her tail and find something new, finally grew past her fear.

Not to mention, the carved-out piece of her heart was out there somewhere. She may have no idea what she should be looking for, but she knew she wouldn't find it in the caverns.

"We are." Lucia slurped down a bright purple thing and flung the shell behind her. It clattered against the rocky wall and fell to the ground. Her voice was different than Lydia's. Rough, lightly slurred.

The redhead leaned back on the oddly shaped benches they sat against. "Do you feel like joining us this time?" She surveyed Lydia, her long fingers absentmindedly running along the ridged scar just above her breast.

"I think so," Lydia murmured. The other women at the table had grown quiet, listening to her talk. "I'd like to get out a bit. See where we are."

Lucia nodded. "I don't know that you're ready to go with the group, but I can take the day to show you around."

A flicker of annoyance went through Lydia's stomach. Her hands clenched against it, an automatic response to avoid showing a hint of her true feelings on her face. She paused, processing her body's reaction to her own emotions.

After a moment she nodded. "I'd like that, thank you."

Lucia smiled. Her shinning white teeth, rosy lips, and wide eyes gave an impression of kindness, but there was something dark behind them. Something Lydia had yet to name. But she recognized it. Recognized the way Lucia's gaze found her each time she sang.

She wondered how close the mermaid was. The one who said she would be watching, waiting for Lydia to make a different choice.

"More?" A young siren, younger than Lydia with a ring of reddened flesh around her pale neck and a permanent smile on her smooth face, offered up a silver platter of multi-colored shelled things.

Lydia couldn't help the smile in return. Tatiana had grown closer and closer to her side since she'd arrived.

"Thank you."

Tatiana rested the plate on the ornately carved wooden table. "You're coming out with us?"

"Not quite," Lydia said.

The girl's face fell. "You'd be such a help. Your voice is so beautiful."

Lydia laughed. "Thank you. Yours is remarkable as well."

Tatiana shrugged. "It's not enough though. I don't contribute much."

Lydia glanced to her left. Lucia had fallen into a conversation with one of the sirens who had fetched her on that first day. The others were finishing their meals, some leaving the table to brush out their flowing hair, rub red onto their lips, or clean their scales.

"What is it you contribute to?" Lydia asked. She kept her face calm, her voice steady, but she lowered the volume ever so slightly.

"You'll see."

Lydia jolted, hand going to her chest as Lucia's head swerved between the two of them, a wide smile on her face.

"Let's see how your tour goes." She held out a hand.

Lydia took it, swallowing at Tatiana's now wide eyes, and allowed Lucia to pull her from the curved stone.

"I think we'll be able to show you *everything* as soon as tomorrow." She smiled as the two of them glided away from the table.

Lydia gave Tatiana a small wave, but the younger girl only returned it with a weak smile.

"That would be lovely," Lydia heard herself say. The words, and grip of Lucia's hand on her wrist, brought not a flash of memory but a surge of emotion, bitter and strong, to the forefront of her being.

She gently tugged, and Lucia released her hand.

"Everything all right?"

Lydia nodded and continued to follow the siren as she collected the things she brought with her during the day. As they went, Lydia frowned. She ran her tongue against her teeth. They'd lost their sharp edged, smoothing down once again to normal, human teeth.

CHAPTER TWENTY

Wire and Steel

Derek and Alyana spent the better part of the next day swimming. Alyana had found a satchel in the wreckage of the ship, and they'd stuffed as much food as would fit inside. The discovery of a barrel of apples and a smaller one of oranges had brought some happiness to what was otherwise a dower morning.

The shell pointed them past the wreck, on toward the shores of Lydia's kingdom. The stories Alyana told, coupled with the already present dangers Derek was aware of in these waters, had him wishing for a longer blade.

It was a few hours from evening when they stopped again to ask the witch's token if they were still on the right track. To both of their surprise, it shifted. As they watched, the simple cream-colored shell rose and pulled at Derek's neck, then halted, moved to the right and up, and pulled again.

"It changed," Alyana whispered, her eyes wide.

Derek nodded. "We're close enough to notice if she moves. That's... that's huge Alyana. We might even find her tonight."

Her smile could have lit the furthest depths of the sea they swam in.

"Up we go." Derek grinned. He was ready for sunlight that wasn't filtered through the water. The darkness below them had grown ever deeper since they'd left the wreck. He took the lead, pumping his powerful tail and gaining speed as the glittering surface drew nearer.

"Derek?"

He slowed only slightly at Alyana's hesitant tone. When he turned his head to look back at her, a shadow caught his sight.

Then a net caught him.

"*No*." Derek's muffled shout was cut short as a tangle of thick wire surrounded him. The shadow, a ship which had come from behind him, passed overhead. There was a lurch. His body jerked against the net, and he stared in horror as Alyana quickly began to fade from view.

"Wait!" she shouted.

Derek's heart raced. He twisted, wriggled, worked against the suffocating net which pressed every inch of him. His tail ached, scrunched at an odd angle against the wire. His fingers grasped at his hilt.

There was no room to draw the blade. He could pull it an inch, just enough to see the glint of steel, but no further.

The opening of the net was above him. He released the hilt, reached up with his other hand, grasped the wire latticework, and hefted.

A split second later he let go of the net with a gasp of pain. Blood gushed from his fingers. He'd gripped the outer edge of the wire, which was now dotted with shreds of his skin.

Other spots of pain took his notice. His adrenaline had blocked a good portion of it, but his back, arms, and tail were all speckled with motes of blood oozing up from the flesh and scales.

He sucked in a shaky breath and shifted his head just enough to look up. The shadow—the ship—above him maintained its course and speed. If it was a fishing vessel, which seemed likely given the net, they'd slow soon enough to unload their haul.

Alyana might be able to figure out a way to free him before the net reached the open air.

If she was anywhere near him. Her shout and the outstretched arm reaching toward him were the last he'd seen of her. The speed of their tails was nothing compared to a ship at full sail.

The tang of his own blood coated his tongue. Derek blinked through the red-tinged water surrounding him.

Surrounding...

The ship had slowed.

There was a painful lurch. His tail twitched at the suffocating pressure.

They were pulling him up.

"*No, no, no.*" Her voice came from below. Anger radiated through the words as Alyana swam into view from the darkness.

She drew her small dagger before she reached him. As the net continued to shift through the water, she began to hack at the wire.

"It's no use," Derek said. His throat stuck, tears burning his eyes. "It's wire. That little blade won't do it."

She snarled at him; teeth bared as she struck again. "You can't breathe up there, Derek."

"I know." He swallowed. A hollow pit of fear ate up his stomach. He pushed it down, forced it away from his heart and mind. "Listen to me."

Alyana growled again. She shifted, grasping at the wire, and leaving pinpricks of blood as she moved around, trying to find a better place to cut.

"Alyana," Derek choked out her name. "We don't have a lot of time."

Indeed, the shadow of the ship had become a hull above them, the lines of the wood finally visible.

He flexed his arms, wincing at the nicks in his skin as he moved. The hand near his hilt was stuck, but with the other he was able to grasp the chord around his neck.

Alyana took one more hack at the wire, punctuating it with a loud grunt. "We have to get you out," she panted.

"Take it," he said. He twisted his head, hissing through his teeth as his ear caught on the wire and the skin ripped.

With trembling flingers, he slipped the chord over his head. "Alyana."

She met his gaze then, her green eyes full of sorrow and rage. "I can't *leave* you here."

Even as she said it, her pale fingers reached for the chord.

"What about Lydia?" she murmured.

Derek grimaced. He struggled again against the wire. He glanced up at the ship.

The ship. The rope being used to pull the net out of the water. Rope. Not wire. Tied to metal hooks at the top of the net, nearly six feet above him. Almost at the surface.

"Alyana."

She followed his gaze.

Alyana released the chord holding the shell. She darted toward the surface, tail pushing her up and up and...

The top of the net breached the water. She sucked in a chest-full of the sea and plowed through the surface.

Derek looped the witch's token back around his neck and watched, helpless. Her tail swished back and forth, keeping her in place. There was a jerk on the net. The speed increased.

Then a corner fell. Another. A third.

As one edge of the net was dragged to the ship, Derek tumbled from the opening. His tail extended. Relief sang through his bones, his muscles, his mind.

He sprung, stretching his arms to the side, and glanced up to find Alyana.

There was the net, the final corner disappearing above the water. Where was she? He scanned the glinting surface for a sign of her tail. The red should have been easy to spot.

He darted up, only a few yards from the ship.

A scream pierced the air above him.

CHAPTER TWENTY-ONE

One of Us

Lydia followed Lucia around the small island where the sirens made their home. According to her guide, the land itself was deserted.

Lydia certainly understood why no one would attempt to reach the island. The thing was surrounded by jagged, fiercely battered rocks. They went deep, forming the caves she'd spent the last few days in.

Lucia kept them away from the bottom, however. The two swam just under the glistening surface of the water as Lucia explained more of what Lydia could expect of her new life.

"It's a bit different for us," Lucia said, flipping onto her back and using her long tail to continue forward while she looked at Lydia. "Mermaids are creatures of the sea once they turn. We have a bit more freedom."

"What do you mean?" Lydia met the siren's gaze. "Surely we can't go on land."

Lucia smiled. "No, these don't come off." She gestured to her tail.

Lydia chuckled.

"Mermaids," Lucia explained, "can't go above the surface. They can't breathe air. If they're up there too long..."

"They suffocate." Lydia's laugh died in her throat. She glanced at the sunlight dancing above them. It looked less like diamonds now, more like edges of blades. "I'm not entirely like you though." Her gaze darted back to Lucia.

The siren shrugged. "Not entirely, but close enough. Your true form, the one that matches the rest of us, will come when you've been here a little longer. If we'd found you first..." Her lips curled into a snarl. "No matter," she said with a wave of her hand. "The choice has been made. You're one of us. It will simply take some time for all the features to present."

She drew her fingers across the intricate wave-like swirls of black tattooed along her shoulders and arms. The others had them too. Younger girls, like Tatiana, only had the beginnings of a pattern. Lucia, who seemed to be the oldest, or at least the one in charge, had black across most of her chest, back, and arms.

"Come," she said. "If you can't breathe above, yet, then we will come back down. If you can..." She put gentle fingers on Lydia's arm. "Then we will sing."

A splash of excitement lit up Lydia's insides. She sucked in a gulp of water and nodded.

Lucia took her hand and pulled her upward. They weren't far from the island. Perhaps a quarter mile from where the rocks began to jut from the surface of the sea. Under them, additional daggers of stone were disguised, covered in algae nearly the color of the water. Lydia hadn't seen much of the seabed yet, but she was sure there were a few sunken ships, unlucky enough to have strayed too close and damaged their hulls.

They broke the surface. Lydia squinted, raising a hand to block her tender eyes from the brightness of the sun. The air was cool against her skin. She held her breath—on instinct—until Lucia gave her a pointed look.

Lydia exhaled, a rush of water easing from her lips as well as the flaps of skin—gills—on her neck.

Lucia watched her, eyes intent.

The air felt strange. Empty and thin, as though they'd reached a great altitude. It took Lydia a few moments of deep breathing to feel like it filled her lungs enough to keep her going.

Lucia's lips split into a grin. "I knew it. This way." She gestured for Lydia to follow, taking a curved path around the rocks toward the far side of the island.

They swam for a while. Though the rocky shore made approach impossible, the island itself seemed to be a lovely place. Beyond the jagged, rock-strewn beaches was dense, lush vegetation. A few birds, in a rainbow of color, darted out to the farthest rocks poking up from the water and back again. The wind picked up. The leaves on the trees danced. Lydia wished she could walk through them.

As much as she'd been drawn to the seaside in her childhood there was nothing she loved so much as a thick forest.

She froze. For a brief second her head slipped below the water before she gave a little shake and worked her tail again.

She liked the forest. Loved it.

Her nose burned, eyes misting as this piece of her memory locked back into place. She glanced at the ring on her finger once more. Something to do. Some mission to fulfill.

Someone missing. A dull ache changed the reason for her tears.

"Almost there," Lucia called over her shoulder.

Lydia jerked. She glanced ahead, where Lucia had continued to swim, not noticing her hesitation. For a brief second, she considered diving down, sinking beneath the waves and… and what? What reason did she have to leave? Where would she even go? The mermaids might take her in, but why? Tatiana seemed nice enough. The others gave her their food, a place to stay. And Lucia… something about Lucia, though demanding and harsh at times, brought Lydia's mind a flicker of memory. Like a forgotten dream.

She exhaled, casting another look at the trees, before hurrying to catch up.

It wasn't much further before they came upon the other sirens. Nearly the entirety of the group Lydia had met, maybe a dozen, hovered off the coast of the island, facing the open sea. A few chatted, but most were silent.

"Are they waiting for something?" Lydia asked.

Lucia nodded. "We think you may be ready."

"Ready?"

"To help. You have unfished business. So do we."

Lydia raised an eyebrow, unease stirring in her chest.

"This is how we settle it." Lucia gestured.

A dot appeared at the edge of the horizon. It took a moment for Lydia to recognize the shape. It was a ship. Dark hull, white sails billowing in the mid-afternoon breeze.

The unease in her chest shifted, roiled and grew and sunk to her stomach as around her, the sirens began to sing.

Chapter Twenty-Two

Can She Breathe

Derek darted toward the ship with fear like ice in his heart. He sucked in a chest-full of water and sprang up from the sea with a splash. The rail was far above him, but he caught sight of a red tail being yanked over the side as another scream filled the air.

Shouts followed it. A few figures gestured over the side of the ship, pointing his way.

Heat built in his chest. Not pain from the lack of breathing. Fury. Intolerable rage as Alyana screamed again.

He dove back down. A spear—no, harpoon—slammed into the water beside him. The rope connected to its end was thin and knotted tight. He caught a brief glance before the thing was yanked back up. He swam to the hull of the ship. Coming up, his gaze darted across the wood. There must be something, some set of cracks, planks, carvings for him to pull himself up with.

There.

One of the portholes—just enough room for his hands to grip the top of the metal seal. His fingers latched around the top and he pulled.

Immediately the realization struck that this would not work. His tail was too heavy. There were no feet for him to use to help climb. Still, he reached for another handhold, a small divot in the wood above him.

A second harpoon sliced across his shoulder. Shouts of triumph sounded above. He lost his grip, fell back, and slammed into the water.

The harpoon floated beside him. He sucked in another breath, drew his sword, and latched his hand around the staff of the harpoon.

They pulled him a few feet from the surface before they realized he was holding the harpoon, rather than impaled on it. They dropped it. He looped the rope around his arm, holding the harpoon in one hand, his sword in the other.

Derek darted beneath the water for another breath. When he came back up, he paused. There was something… voices on the air.

The sailors had disappeared from the rail of the ship. A few were still visible in the rigging, but he couldn't see the ones who'd been after him. Nor could he see Alyana.

He snarled, anger escalating as the ship's sails caught the breeze and it began to move faster. He sheathed his weapon and swam. His tail pumped hard, the muscles protesting such aggressive movements.

He followed it, praying to the gods of the sea that Alyana didn't suffocate. Her eyes were still different than his. Maybe her lungs were different as well.

A bitter grimace twisted across his lips. If not...

No.

She would not die like this. Not for saving him.

He kept pace with the ship, swimming alongside it. Every few dozen yards he returned to the surface. The singing grew louder. As did chatter from the deck of the ship. He didn't hear Alyana screaming anymore, and the lack of her voice sent another wave of cold fear through his veins.

He tried to call to her once, but the only sound that came out was an odd gurgling. He'd lost his voice as well as his ability to breathe.

It didn't take long for the ship's new course to become clear. Ahead of them, visible even under the surface, a small island came into view. Derek popped his head up again. The singing had grown loud enough to drown the sound of the wind upon the sea. The sailors on the ship were hollering, shouting, and waving their hands. A few had taken off their shirts and now stood atop the rigging and rails, whistling and cheering.

Something pulled at Derek's neck. He went back under, glancing down. The shell no longer rested against his chest. It hovered ahead of him. As fast as he was swimming, whatever magic moved the shell was faster. It pulled him forward.

The singing, the sailors, and the shell all clicked into place in his frazzled brain. Daunting realization hit, and he suffered a brief bout of helplessness. He drifted, letting the shell yank at his neck until the skin there chaffed.

The ship went on, the end passing him. He blinked. There, dangling from the back, forgotten by the besotted fools on board, was a thick line of rope.

He swallowed. Lydia might be too late to save, but Alyana would not suffer at the hands of the sailors. Besides, it would be imprudent not to take advantage of a perfect distraction.

He darted forward. His fingers curled around the rope, the harpoon hanging from its own chord around his arm.

Derek winced. His arms jerked in their sockets as the speed of the ship gave his tail a break but nearly pulled his arms apart. He held on. Before them, only a few hundred yards in front of the ship, a massive rock formation was taking shape.

The stones were similar to the ones in the sea witch's cave, a familiar dark black with jutting edges. The formation sank, deeper than Derek could see, and also rose above the surface of the water. Surely the men above could see it...

He shook his head, fury curdling into absolute lack of pity as he pulled himself up the rope.

CHAPTER TWENTY-THREE

Where You Belong

"What are you doing?" Lydia demanded.

A few of the sirens eyed her for a second, but their voices never wavered. The song was low, lilting, and beautiful. She longed to join it. Her chest expanded with breath, ready.

She swallowed down the urge, her gaze flicking from the ship fast approaching to Lucia beside her. The siren's voice was even more stunning now than it had been during those simple songs in the caves.

Memories stirred in Lydia's mind. Myths, legends, stories of sea creatures... beings like the ones around her.

"You can't do this." She grabbed Lucia's arm.

The chorus of voices went short one. The redhead turned to meet Lydia's eye. "Can't do *what*?"

Lydia removed her hand. "You're going to crash the ship," Lydia said, her lips barely parted as the crushing weight of fear and guilt coiled within her. "You plan to kill them?"

Lucia raised an eyebrow. "Indeed. This is what we do, Lydia. I thought you were ready."

Lydia shook her head, locks of black hair dangled around her shoulders. "I... I want no part of this. I'm leaving."

She ducked under the water, spinning away from the collection of tails visible under the surface. She made it a few feet before tight fingers grasped her upper arm.

"I don't think so." Lucia's voice grew harsh, dark. "You made your choice. You belong with us now. That voice of yours is too powerful to let go."

Heat flared in Lydia's chest. She jerked out of Lucia's grip, her lips pinched together in anger. "I was in no condition to make any decision. What you're doing here is *wrong*. I will not help you."

Lucia snarled. Her teeth grew sharp. The tattoos across her skin shifted, waves of black moving across her flesh. "The sailors on that ship are *men*. Have men not hurt you? Used you? Done you wrong time and again?"

"I..." Lydia swallowed. "I won't stay here."

Lucia's eyes glinted with hints of red. Her hair billowed behind her. The very sea seemed to grow colder. "I see that ring on your finger, the crown of pearls you left behind on the ocean floor. Tell me princess. Tell me it was *your* choice to marry whoever gave you that ring. Tell me that honestly, and I'll let you go."

Behind Lucia, the bottom hull of the ship raced towards them. Lydia's hands clenched into fists. This is what it was... what it always was. No choice. Only control. She glanced at the ring. She looked up at the ship, so close now that the sirens above them had scattered to the sides, giving room for the hull to destroy itself upon the rocks.

"Stay with us, princess." Lucia's voice drifted in, haunting, dark. "Stay with us where you belong."

"Never," Lydia muttered. She twisted the ring, watching the ship behind Lucia. "I've never belonged. And I certainly don't with you."

A low growl sounded through the water. Lucia's nails lengthened, her blackened fingers becoming talons as she darted for Lydia with terrifying speed.

At that moment, the ship hit the rocks.

The force of it blew both of them backward. Lydia spun, head over tail, until she rammed into a jagged rock and floated there, stunned. A few seconds passed before she was able to shake her head. Bringing herself to the present, she gazed around, searching for Lucia.

There, drifting through the water a few yards below. Lydia almost swam down to check if the siren was alive, but then her tail twitched. Her eyes fluttered open. She caught sight of Lydia.

Lydia's dark eyes widened, and she bolted.

Chunks of ship were strewn around them. Bodies drifted above. Some men swam toward the island, vain attempts to find land. Others swam down, their gazes glassy and fixed on the sirens who had ducked beneath the water.

Lydia swerved around a set of chains, sinking fast into the deep. She glanced behind her. Lucia had paused. Her talons were locked around a man, fingers raking through his short brown hair. She met Lydia's eye, curled her lips in a threatening smile, and sank her teeth into the man's shoulder.

Lydia's stomach lurched. The man struggled, the hypnotism lost as Lucia pulled a chunk of flesh from where his shoulder and neck met. Lydia's hand flew to her lips in horror. The man fought, scratching at the thing before him, bubbles escaping from his near-silent screams. His efforts made no impact on the siren.

Lucia kept her gaze fixed on Lydia as she chewed, swallowed, and went in for another bite. By the time she'd lowered her mouth again, the man's body had gone limp. Blood stained the water a dark, ruddy brown as she took another chunk from his flesh.

Lydia swallowed the bile rising in her throat, turned tail, and fled.

Lucia's voice cackled behind her. "You won't get far, princess. You belong to us now. We *will* find you."

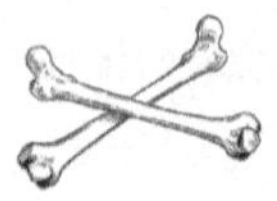

CHAPTER TWENTY-FOUR

Blood, Bones, and Bubbles

Derek had mere moments at the most. He knew this as his head broke the water, wind cold on his skin. It was lucky he was behind the bulk of the ship, or the chill would have frozen him to the bone.

He pulled. His tail helped propel him a few extra feet before it dangled behind, an empty weight. His fingers reached the wooden rial of the ship. Every inch of his arms burned, his muscles aching as he hefted. He latched an elbow over the side, his lungs burning now too.

He glanced ahead and wished he could suck in a breath.

His lips parted at the sight before him; water dribbled down his chin. The sailors had abandoned their posts. All of them, maybe two dozen men, scrambled toward the front of the ship. They shouted, jostled, pushed each other, clamoring to be first to see, first to touch. They pointed excitedly at something... something in the water.

None noticed the towering stone coming toward them.

Derek scanned the deck. There, against the rail at the mid-point of the ship.

Alyana.

She was alive, breathing. Blood marked her skin and tail, the dark red of it only visible by the missing scales which left black oozing pockets.

She'd crawled, judging by the streaks of red on the wood. Reached the side.

Derek exhaled in relief, more water flowing from the gills on his neck.

The ship hit the rocks.

Derek flew backward as the ship scrunched, and then folded. Wood splintered and crashed around him. He hit the water, pain reverberating through his back and tail.

Inhaling relieved the burning in his lungs. He flicked his tail, turned, and headed straight for the worst of the wreckage. Bits of splintered wood hit him as he swam, searching.

Bodies filled the water. Men, knocked overboard. Some swam toward the shore. One moved right past Derek without seeming to notice him at all. The man's eyes were glazed over, his focus hazy. He wasn't trying to reach the surface, Derek realized.

Derek shrugged past the unease growing in him, moved around the man, and continued to scan the water for Alyana.

She had to be here. She'd been so close to the edge...

"*Alyana!*" Derek shouted into the odd stillness of the wreck.

When his ship had gone down a storm had raged. This was different. A sunny day, barely a cloud. The world shimmered with light, shafts growing and fading as bits of the ship cast shadows through the water.

He caught a glimpse of red hair and darted forward. She was drifting. Floating, as still as sleep, her eyes closed.

He swam, his gaze catching for a brief second on the main mast of the ship. It left a trail of bubbles as it sank down... down... heading straight for Alyana's torso.

Derek pushed, the pain in his body reached a breaking point as he went faster than he'd though possible. One arm closed around Alyana's pale shoulders, the other tucked under her tail. He kept moving, straight forward as the mast whispered past his scales.

He grunted as a force slammed into his shoulder. A man. Swimming without thought or care as he made toward the island rocks. Another piece of wood came swirling down through the water. Derek shouted. The man didn't hear—or didn't care. The chunk of wood slammed into him, pulling him to the depths.

Derek swallowed. Blood and death surrounded him. He clenched Alyana tight to his chest, turned from the island, and dove.

The sea floor surrounding the island was coated in the remnants of sunken ships. The sand below was almost completely covered, some hulls stacked two or three high.

Derek skirted the ragged rocks as a chunk of the ship that had just crashed reached the bottom. It slammed down. A spray of splinters, chunks of wood, and bone spiraled outward.

Derek turned, shielding Alyana's body as a heavy board slammed across his back.

He shouted in pain.

A slice split across his shoulder blade, blood seeping from the wound. He grunted, gritted his teeth, and continued around the side of the island.

He should leave. Should heave Alyana across his shoulder and swim as far away from this as he could. But the shell around his neck was alight. It glowed with a warm yellow light, no longer dangling by the chord but up, floating. Pulling Derek forward. Each time he turned, swerved to avoid falling debris, it turned as well; like a compass keeping a northward bearing. But this wasn't taking him north. It was taking him to Lydia.

Running was his favored option. The sirens had just murdered an entire ship of men. Granted, he had no pity for the beasts who had nearly captured him and *had* hurt Alyana, but as he passed dozens of wreckages, he wondered how many innocent souls had been dragged beneath the sea by the beautiful voices he'd heard.

Down he went, further from the endless ripples of bubbles stemming up from freshly drowned wood and men. A pull caught his attention. He paused, far enough from the wreckage that he didn't fear another strike from the sinking ship.

The chord heated his neck, friction from the vibrating shell as it yanked him, pointing the way forward.

Lydia was close.

CHAPTER TWENTY-FIVE

A Flash of Red

Fear kept her moving, but with no notion of where she could go to escape the sirens, Lydia found herself swimming deeper. She'd escaped the muddy red water. Escaped the bodies, the men who'd grasped at her hair and tail as she'd passed, even as their lungs filled with water, the last of their air escaping in tendrils of pearls reaching for the surface.

Lydia now understood why Lucia had kept her near the surface of the island. The sea floor was littered with broken ships. She spotted a few dark fins, shuddered, and hurried on. By the time she'd reached the far side of the little island, her heart had calmed.

She could flee, making for open water and try to find... what? Mermaids? They might not be killers, but who was to say? Who was to say they'd take her in now? After...

A shudder ripped through her from the base of her neck to the tip of her tail. Bile rose in her throat at the fresh memory of Lucia biting into that sailor's flesh.

She wasn't. She *wouldn't* be a siren.

Something shifted above her. A shadow in the water.

She ducked out of sight, preferring the threat of sharks to the sirens finding her. She'd hoped they were busy—her stomach recoiled—eating. Hoped she had some time to figure out a plan of escape. Clearly not.

Lydia grasped a fallen mast, the broken end a few feet above her, sail dangling limply onto the sand below. She watched, shrunk down into her hiding place, as a bulky figure swam overhead.

No. Two figures.

A flash of red pulled her. Like a chain tied to her rib bones, it tugged her out from the wreckage. Her brow furrowed, fingers twisting the ring on her finger around and around.

Curiosity and confusion swirled as she realized one of the figures was male presenting. They pulled past her, swimming onward until, though she made no noise, the one with short blonde hair and a long blue tail halted.

He flicked his tail. Turned.

A seashell glowed at his neck, stretched out as though it was reaching toward her. When their eyes met, the shell went dark and dropped to his chest. His skin was smooth, lightly tan, and delicate apart from a smattering of fresh cuts. No sight of the scars she'd grown accustomed too on the sirens.

His eyes were mermaid-like, but... he couldn't be either creature, could he?

The thoughts lasted a second, barley. For as he turned, the flash of red became visible in the figure he was carrying.

Lydia's lips parted in a brief exhale. A woman—siren? But again, without the scars. And this one had tied a ripped dress over herself the same way Lydia had, the ends of the fabric just brushing the top of her tail. Her pale skin glistened like the moon.

A surge of memory bent Lydia at the waist, fingers digging through her locks to clutch her aching skull. Moonlight. Pale fingers, drifting across her skin. A voice asking, always *asking*, for her to sing.

One more, please?

Lydia gasped a breath and slowly straightened, one hand on her chest, the other hanging limp at her side. "I... I know you."

The man shifted closer. He kept a few yards between them, his gaze wary. "Indeed. We've been searching for you, Lydia."

She blinked. Her eyes left him for a moment, still caught on the woman in his arms. "Were you... were you on the ship?"

He nodded.

"You drowned."

A grimace flashed across his face. "No. I'm so sorry about what happened, Lydia. I wanted to... I wish we'd have found you before you had to go through that. But no, we didn't drown." He glanced at the redhead he carried, concern replacing the grimace.

"Is she…"

"She'll be all right," he murmured. "We had a time finding you, but she won't care."

Lydia frowned. She swished her tail, pushing back through the water a few feet even as the invisible chord in her chest yearned for her to go toward them. "*Finding me?*"

"I'm not," he swallowed, "I'm not explaining it right. We've been worried about what we might find when we finally got to you."

His gaze went past her then, back toward the song and bloodshed she'd fled.

"A siren."

He nodded again. "It was a concern, but you don't seem to want to eat me." His weak half-smile almost brought one to her lips as well. "So that's a good sign."

"Why though?" Lydia's body trembled. She clenched her fists, trying to get it to stop. The fear, the tension, the anger, it had built to a head and finally crashed over her like a wave. Exhaustion dragged at her bones. "Why come for me?"

He opened his mouth, then closed it again. After a moment he drifted forward and murmured, "Lydia, what do you remember?"

CHAPTER TWENTY-SIX

True Love

Derek's arms ached. Alyana wasn't a particularly heavy individual, but after hauling himself up the side of that ship he was ready to set her down. Add the slice in his shoulder blade, the man-eating siren's, and the shark fins he'd seen lurking in the wreckage below... he was done being in the sea. Land sounded good. Land, food, and clothes.

But Alyana's fears about Lydia's memory had proved real. As much as he wanted to go back to his kingdom, he was pretty sure love's true kiss couldn't be planted on someone by a complete stranger.

"I..." Lydia shook her head, dark locks drifting in the water behind her. "I don't remember much of anything, really. Just feelings."

He glanced down at Alyana. "You remember her?"

Lydia shook her head again, slower this time, a hesitant look crossing her features. "I don't... but I want to."

He met her gaze. There was longing in her eyes.

"I want to remember her."

Derek blew out a sigh. "It might help if she were awake."

"What happened to you?" The concern in her voice drove an ache through his chest.

"We found out you weren't gone. Not, you know, really gone. So, we found a way to get you back."

"No." She held up a hand and shook her head.

He froze in place as she moved toward them. Her fingers brushed the scratches on Alyana's arms. Her eye traveled to the spots of missing scales on Alyana's tail.

"This. What happened?"

Derek swallowed. "That ship." He jerked his chin behind her, back toward the wreckage and feasting sirens. "It caught me in a net. A strange one, wire. Alyana cut me out, but they took her when she did."

"*Alyana.*" She said it like a breath. Like the word itself was as delicate as a glass flower. "Alyana."

He nodded. "I'm Derek. You and I..." The words locked in his throat. "Alyana is your handmaiden. Your friend. You and she were on a ship with me, coming to my kingdom. A storm caught us."

Lydia nodded. Her hand hadn't moved from Alyana's arm. "I remember. The storm," she corrected at his look. "I remember the storm." Her head tilted as she studied the unconscious woman in his arms. "And I remember..."

"Would you..." Derek gritted his teeth. The pain in his body was settling deeper the longer they floated there.

"Would you try to wake her? I don't think we should stay here much longer."

Lydia's eyes went wide. She glanced at him, then back the way they'd come. Her jaw tightened and she nodded. Her fingers moved, brushing a strand of hair that had come loose from Alyana's braid.

"Alyana." She tried the word again, almost like she was testing the way it rolled across her tongue.

In his arms, Alyana stirred.

Lydia's fingers stroked her forehead. "Alyana," she said again. "I need your help. I need you to wake up and help me remember."

Alyana's eyelids fluttered. The steady rise and fall of her chest shifted. She sucked in a gulp of water. Her hand flew to Derek's arm, fingers digging into his skin for a moment.

She sat up, and he released her, though she still clung to him. She floated beside him for a moment, wincing as her tail unfurled below her. Flecks of blood oozed from the missing scales. "Bastards," she spat. "They kept poking it."

Derek brushed his hand across hers. She looked up. Her gaze met his. He looked toward Lydia.

Alyana gasped. Her hands flew to her mouth. She darted forward but stopped. Hesitated a just in front of Lydia, holding her breath.

"Lydee?"

Lydia's eyes were wide. Dark circles of fear, confusion, and a glint... a flicker of recognition. Her lips parted. The furrow in her brow smoothed. She uttered the smallest sound, a single note before her hands reached toward Alyana.

"Aly..."

Derek flicked his tail, backing a few feet away to give them a bit of space.

A sob broke from Alyana's chest as Lydia moved forward, arms wide. The two embraced, holding each other tight for several long moments. When they finally broke apart, Alyana looked to Derek with reddened eyes.

"You found her."

He shrugged a shoulder, flicking his tail out as he did to avoid listing to the side. "The shell found her."

Alyana went to him, tugging Lydia along as their fingers were still tightly entwined, and gave him a one-armed hug.

"Thank you," she murmured into his ear.

He closed an arm around her, squeezing back. "Thank *you*. You saved me, Alyana."

She pulled away with a wry grin. "I needed to you get to her." She folded both hands over Lydia's.

"Right," Derek chuckled.

"What do you..." Alyana grimaced. She faced Lydia, tilting her head. "What do you remember?"

Lydia smiled. "More. Not everything, but I remember you." Her hand cupped Alyana's cheek. "I remember this." She lifted her hand, showing them both the ring Derek had picked out months ago. "And I remember what I was supposed to do."

She lifted her chin and turned to Derek.

Beside her, Alyana's breath caught. She looked to Derek as well, pain and determination flashing through her green eyes. "Of course. Derek, it's time. Break the spell. Send us back to land."

Lydia frowned. "There's a way back?"

Alyana nodded, a tight smile on her lips. "Derek made a deal. He delivers true love's kiss, and we all get to go home. You get to live again." She chuckled. "With legs."

Lydia glanced at her tail, then at Derek. "That's it? A kiss and we leave the sea?"

He nodded. "You make it sound simple, but we also had to find you. And we only had three days."

"Speaking of which," Alyana grumbled with a pointed look at him. "Aren't we nearing the end of that deadline?"

Derek grinned. "We are." He looked at the princess. "Lady Lydia, with your permission?"

She straightened at the name, her chin rising, shoulders going back. Alyana brushed a lock of Lydia's hair behind her shoulder. Lydia gave Derek a single, solemn nod.

She held out a hand. He took it. Alyana released Lydia, wringing her fingers together as she looked away.

"Alyana?" Derek raised an eyebrow and cocked his head at her.

"What?" She frowned at him, confusion on her face.

"Well, I sort of need you for this part."

"What do you..."

He took her hand, bringing the two women on either side of him. He met Alyana's eye, an easy smile on his lips. "The witch said I had to *deliver* true love's kiss. That's what I'm doing." He brought their hands together, winked at his friend, and backed away.

The happiness that shone through Lydia's eyes in that moment might have blinded him, but he was busy looking at Alyana. She kept his gaze for a long moment, watching him move back with disbelief on her face. Finally, lips trembling, she mouthed, "*thank you.*"

"I told you we'd find her. Now, get us home."

Chapter Twenty-Seven

Golden Kisses

A storybook kiss is often short. A brush of lips. Sometimes on a sleeping figure—gross. Sometimes it goes long, passionate, and heated.

This wasn't a storybook kiss Derek had ever read. The love between the women before him simultaneously filled him and left him empty. Alyana's hand slid to the back of Lydia's head, fingers coiling in her black locks. Lydia's arms closed around Alyana's waist, making little divots in the pale skin with her fingers.

Their lips met with all the heat and softness of a warm fire on a winter's night. Pure and right and good and everything that would make snow melt, hearts soften, and love sing through the air.

Indeed, as the kiss deepened and Derek averted his gaze, singing filled the water around them. Not the haunting melody he'd heard as the ship careened toward the shore. This was something...

He gasped as light sparked. Between the women, arcs of gold sprang from the where their lips met. Strands of it enveloped them, cocooning them in glinting brightness. A few strands flew to him as well. They poked at him, and he swore he heard a chuckle before the golden light caressed his cheeks.

Heat rushed his veins. Pain ached through his tail. He closed his eyes against the light, bright enough to burn.

When the blazing light behind his eyelids faded, replaced with a softer, duller red, he squinted them open.

Then he fell down.

He gaped, staring wide-eyed at the feet at the end of his legs. Legs and feet and an ass he'd just fallen on. Dirt beneath his hands. Well, sand, but dirty sand. The kind found on the shore.

He was—thankfully—fully clothed. The sword at his belt remained intact. Even his hair was dry. He rolled his shoulders. The gash on his back had either healed or disappeared the same way his tail had. Even the multitude of scrapes along his arms had been replaced with smooth skin.

It took a few minutes for him to climb to his feet. It was like having sea legs, but ten times worse. He couldn't figure out which way his toes were supposed to wiggle, until he realized he didn't usually actively control his toes.

In focusing on something else, his feet figured themselves out without the need for much help from him.

After he'd stood, dusted off his pants, and taken several painless gulps of salty sea air, he realized where he was.

Derek stood at the edge of a gently rolling cliff. Sand, seaweed, driftwood, and a collection of shells littered the beach. A gnarled set of dark rocks climbed from the water a good ways in. A soft smile parted his lips.

She'd kept her end of the deal.

It was tempting, to go back down, wade into the sea, and visit her. Find out if she knew the whole time what was going on. If she was watching them somehow. Or if it was just the magic of their bargain that had gotten them back.

Derek felt for the chord at his neck. It was still there, thick and sticky with salt. He tugged the shell free from under his shirt. It hung down to his sternum. He grinned, brushing a thumb across it before turning away from the water.

Derek moved away from the cliff, back toward the gently blowing fields of green and the dirt path that led to the small inn where he and Alyana had left their horses.

He wandered for a minute, anxiety rising as he didn't immediately spot the princess or her handmaiden. Then he came around a particularly thick oak tree to find them continuing the passionate kiss that had gotten them all home. He gaped for a split second, wheeled back around, and strolled back to the cliff.

Derek sat, blushing to the roots of his hair. They'd been gone nearly three days. He could wait another few hours before they returned to the castle. In the meantime, he'd plan what to say to his father. He stared out at the sea, watching waves in the distance crash, white foam building on the sand.

It was not going to be a fun conversation.

CHAPTER TWENTY-EIGHT

Not a Wish

It was not a fun conversation.

Derek, Lydia, and Alyana had been greeted at the city gates. The guards had taken one look at the missing crown prince before nearly pouncing him. With one man holding each arm, and a third walking behind the women, they were marched to the palace.

Derek's scoffs that this was "highly unnecessary" and that he was "rescuing a princess" fell on deaf ears. It seemed his father's reaction to his leaving had been rather harsher than he'd anticipated.

Charles met them at the palace doors.

The second in line for the throne waved away the guards, insisting that he be the one to walk them before the king. The men agreed and released their grips on the crown prince, but they stayed on either side, wary eyes on him as though he were a bolting foal.

"To be fair," Charles muttered with a grin after Derek mentioned this. "You basically are."

"I rescued a princess, brother," Derek grumbled.

Charles laughed. He glanced behind them where Lydia and Alyana walked along, faces bright, hands clenched together. "Indeed, you did. I didn't... I didn't want to hope. But I'm proud of you." His gaze flicked to the family portrait on the wall as they walked past. "Mother would be proud as well."

"Father on the other hand..." Derek raised an eyebrow.

"Oh, you're not ready for it." Charles shook his head. "He's furious. Never seen him like this. Milk it that you're back. Take advantage of the fact that you didn't actually die, and the marriage can go on as planned. He'll be grateful for the treaty staying intact."

Derek hesitated and put a hand on his brother's elbow, drawing their party to a halt. He glanced back, catching Alyana's gaze for a brief second.

"About that, Charles."

Charles' eyes widened. He glanced at the women as well, finally taking in their hands, the way Lydia was staring at Alyana with unabashed, unfiltered love in her expression.

"Ahh." He pinched the bridge of his nose. "Derek—"

"I'll not marry her, Charles." Derek met his brother's eye with a fierce gaze. "I'll not put them through that."

Charles swallowed. He grimaced. He clenched his teeth, bit his lip, and ran a hand through his dark brown hair, staring at the picture of their mother on the wall. "Yeah."

He closed his eyes with a sigh. "I'll back you up, Derek. But this is, somehow, going to go even worse than I imagined."

Derek threw an arm around his brother's shoulders. "I'm alive, that's got to count for something, right?"

They continued on. The guards pulled apart the double doors, and a herald announced their arrival.

Given the state of the court he needn't have bothered.

Derek's father, the king, sat on the throne at the end of the room. Chandeliers dangled every few yards, their light only necessary after sunset. Massive glass windows took up the entire wall behind the king. Golden arches maintained the structure; above them little pockets of stained glass sent shoots of color onto the marble floor.

Courtiers stood on either side as Derek, his brother, and the rest of their little group walked toward the throne. Whispers echoed through the room. A few of Derek's friends gave him fleeting grins. Looks that said they were grateful he was alive and feared for his coming punishment.

Derek said nothing as they came to the dais and the throne. It was a comfortable thing, thick cushions, and a small golden pillow to support the king's back. A second, wider throne sat to the right of the king's, a few inches back. The queen had commissioned them. One for the king, one for her and the children to share. She always disapproved of leaving them out of important business.

How will they learn to run a kingdom if they cannot watch you do it? She'd asked their father once.

It might have been the only time Derek had seen him speechless. The thrones had been ordered the following day.

Derek bowed low, his brother copying the movement, and the women behind him sinking into deep curtseys as well. Then he straightened, raised his chin, and met his father's gaze.

A moment passed in silence.

"Well," the king said, his lips barely moving. "What do you have to say for yourself, boy?"

Derek bristled at the term, only used when his father felt the need to make him feel like a child. His face remained clear, however.

He inhaled. "Majesty, I can only apologize for not obtaining your blessing before embarking on the journey to rescue my fiancé."

A ripple went through the court. The king held up a well decorated hand. Silence fell.

He stared at Derek, blue eyes meeting blue, before the hint of a smile flickered at the corner of his mouth. "Just like your mother." He shook his head, bemusement replacing the fury that had clouded his gaze. "Asking forgiveness instead of permission."

A smile slid across Derek's lips. "She taught us well," he murmured.

"And roping your brother into it?" his father demanded. "He was telling more lies than I've heard in a decade to cover for you."

Beside him, Charles snorted once before regaining his composure.

"To be fair." Derek took a step toward his father, hands open at his sides. "If any were about mermaids, they weren't lies. I have quite a story to tell you."

"I'm sure you do." The king nodded. "However, it will have to wait. The wedding has been held off long enough. Let's get it on with so we can send word back to Lady Lydia's family that this whole ordeal is done. I'm sure they've suffered in grief long enough."

Derek's smile shifted. "Sire, I might ask for an audience with you before we go forward with the marriage."

The king frowned. "What could you possibly need to discuss? You're here, your fiancé is here. The wedding will commence, and our alliance will grow stronger than it already is."

"Father, please," Derek murmured.

Another round of hissing filled the chamber.

The king's eyes darkened. His lip curled as he surveyed the crown prince. "What reason could you have for causing more unrest in this land?" he asked through clenched teeth.

"I cannot marry her, your Majesty." Derek swallowed. He glanced over his shoulder. Lydia stood frozen, her eyes wide with fear. Beside her, Alyana's knuckles were white, though there was little fear to find on her face.

"You can. And you will."

Derek licked his lips and inhaled. Charles put a hand on his shoulder.

"I will not."

The king's face went red. Anger flashed across his gaze. His hands clenched on the armrests of his throne. "Very well. We will send her back to her land and you will find another wife. Her family can't be too angry, she's alive after all, which is more than they expect at this point."

Derek let out a shaking breath. "I'm afraid we cannot do that either, father. Lady Lydia must leave here free from her family and ours."

"You'd tell a king what *must* happen?" his father growled.

"I'd tell my father what is *right*," Derek replied. Fear gripped his chest. He swallowed as yet more voices rose at this. Murmurs spread through the room.

"Sire," Lydia spoke up, hushing the voices around them. She stepped forward, Alyana sticking to her side. "Your son rescued me from a fate worse than death. That is what he offers me now as well. Returning to my kingdom, my family..." She swallowed. "They are not like you. They know not mercy or forgiveness. My life will not be my own if I am sent back."

Derek's father closed his eyes as he sucked in a breath. "I'm afraid, child, that the consequences of my son's actions are what they are, regardless of what happens to you because of them. If you two refuse to marry, you must go back. We cannot—I *will not*—endanger my people and my kingdom by risking the alliance we have spent decades forging with your uncle."

He waved a hand. On either side of them the guards moved in.

"Father." Derek held up his hands. "Please *listen* to me."

"You are the *crown prince*." The king stood. "You will obey me. And when I tell you the choice is either to marry the princess or send her back and find another, *you* will listen."

Derek's palms were damp as the guards stepped closer. He glanced at his brother. "Would you forgive me, if I did something now that would forever change your life?"

Charles frowned.

Derek's hand went to the chord at his throat. His fingers wrapped around the shell, and he snapped it loose of his neck.

"I..." Charles studied Derek's face. After a pause, he nodded. "I want you to be happy, Derek. I want our family to be happy. Our kingdom to thrive."

"Would you take the throne to make that happen? Would it suffocate you, like it's suffocating me?"

Charles exhaled, pain splashing across his face. "Brother, I'd relieve you of this burden in a heartbeat, but such things cannot be done. You were born first, no matter how much we may wish it different."

On the dais, the king shook with fury. His voice rose, trying to gather the attention of his sons. The royal guards surrounded their party.

Charles glanced at him, but Derek put a hand on his arm. "This, little brother, isn't a wish. It's a bargain."

He looked to Alyana for a split second. Her eyes went wide, mouth opening, but it was too late.

He slammed the shell onto the marble ground. It shattered on impact, shards scattering across the floor.

CHAPTER TWENTY-NINE

The Crown Prince

Light split the room. A whirling vortex of salty air and stinging sand and the sparkle of sunlight on water overtook them all.

As fast as it started, it was done. Derek's hand rested on Charles' arm, next to an intricate golden emblem stitched into his tunic that hadn't been there before. Odd.

Odder still was the woman before them. Tall, slender, and stunning. Black hair cascaded to her waist, smooth like silk. Her dress flowed out behind her, a thing of black and silver, encrusted with pearls and diamonds. A tiara of sapphires rested on her brow. She faced Derek, brown eyes glistening, a smile revealing dazzlingly white teeth.

He frowned. She was familiar. Familiar and yet...

The king was shouting. His gaze found the woman, and he went still. Silent as the woman turned. And, as she did, a hint of yellow in her eyes drew a grin out of Derek.

"Majesty," the woman murmured.

The court went quiet. The guards, who Derek expected to launch at the stranger in their midst, shifted back to their positions before the dais, as though the woman had been there the entire time.

"Who is that?" Charles whispered out the corner of his mouth.

"I'll expl—" Derek began, but he halted as he looked at his brother. Charles stood beside him, a crown resting on his dark coiled hair where none had been merely a second ago.

"Might I suggest a congratulations for your son's valiant rescue of these two women." Symphonia's voice echoed through the chamber. "It is a terrible sadness the princess was lost, but I am sure Crown Prince Charles shall find another suitable bride."

Murmurs of agreement, nods of approval—utterly bewildering to Derek—rippled through the room. He glanced to Alyana and Lydia. They still stood together, but their image shifted, warped. He squinted as though he was looking through the horrible heat of a mid-summer sun.

Lydia no longer stood straight and tall. Her back was slouched, her clothes lesser quality. Alyana looked the same, her handmaiden's outfit matching Lydia's.

Derek gaped for a second before turning back to Charles. His brother stared at him. Charles' fingers went to his forehead, to the crown on his brow.

"Oh," he murmured. An exhale of shock, followed by a slow grin, creeping across his face. "Derek? Is this… is this real?"

Derek nodded. "I believe it is, brother."

The two spoke in hushed tones. Ahead of them, Symphonia had captivated the king. The two of them chatted, nodding and laughing as the court joined along. Only the two princes and the women next to them were silent.

Charles went still for a long moment. Derek's brow furrowed in concern. The burden Charles had just inherited was not an easy one. Finally, at a break in the chuckles being shared among the court, Charles turned to the dais.

"Your Majesty?"

The king held up a hand. Symphonia bowed her head, falling silent as the rest of the room went quiet.

"Charles?"

"I wondered if you'd permit me to study the map and begin my search for a new bride?"

A startled look danced across their father's features. "Well, of course. I must say, I'm glad you're so ready to find someone. Let me know when you've narrowed down a few suitable options."

Charles gave a low bow. As the king turned back to Symphonia, he spoke again. "Might I suggest prince Derek accompany the handmaidens to their ship?"

"Yes, yes." The king waved his hand, unconcerned with Derek in a way he'd never been before.

Derek glanced at his brother.

"Come on," Charles muttered. "Before he changes his mind."

The two princes, with handmaidens in tow, hurried from the chamber.

"We aren't going back." Alyana faced Charles as the doors closed behind them. "We can't. I don't care what magic the witch has, if Lydia is seen in that kingdom..."

"I wouldn't dream of it," Charles said.

Alyana and Lydia exchanged surprised looks. "But you said—"

"It's called lying, dears." Charles chuckled. "Father doesn't bother with the day to day, he won't care if you're on a merchant ship headed for our trade partner or not. As far as your family knows, and apparently *our* entire court, you died at sea," he said to Lydia.

Derek stepped toward the women, his heart heavy. He reached for Alyana's hand, and she gave it. "Take the horses," he murmured. "Go south, there will be plenty of jobs to find along the coast. Plenty of towns where no one will look twice at the two of you. As I told you, our kingdom is quite different from yours. The south is where mother had the most influence. It'll be safe there."

"And," Charles interjected, "you will always have a voice here as well. If you need anything, do not hesitate to ask. I doubt *I'll* be able to meet with you." He grinned. "But this one," he nudged Derek with his shoulder, "can talk to just about anyone now."

Alyana's lips trembled. She squeezed Derek's hand. "I can't... I don't know how to thank you for this."

He shook his head, glancing at Lydia. "I didn't do anything, Alyana. You saved each other, remember?"

She let out a tearful chuckle, shaking her head even as she snaked an arm around Lydia's waist and pulled her close.

"Princess," Derek murmured to Lydia. "It might be a bit much to ask, but might I have that back?"

It was her turn to let out a laugh and, as she did, Charles exhaled and straightened, his eyes wide. Derek grinned at his brother's reaction. Her voice really was something magical.

"Of course," Lydia said. She slid the ring off her finger and passed it to Derek. "Thank you. For delivering her to me."

Derek nodded.

The two women strode down the hall, through the wide-open palace doors, and on to their freedom.

With a furrow in his brow, Derek turned to Charles.

CHAPTER THIRTY

The End

Derek stared at his brother. Once younger brother, but he wasn't quite sure how that worked now. Charles was watching the open palace doors, a wistful expression on his face.

"Well." Charles sighed and rubbed his hands together. "What about you then?"

Derek shook his head, following as his brother strode down the long hall. "Have I just made your life miserable?" he asked.

"Not at all," Charles said. He came to a stop midway and looked to the painting of their family hung on the wall.

"You're certain," Derek insisted. "I've just locked you in the palace for much of the rest of your life."

"Remarkable..." Charles murmured.

Derek frowned, then turned to look at the painting as well. Their mother and father looked the same. The baby's laugh, the children on the floor, all the way it had been a few days ago. The brothers, however...

Derek leaned in, tilting his head as he took in the dark-haired boy that had replaced him in the image. Their father's hand now rested on Charles' shoulder, with Derek looking up at his older brother with that admiring expression.

"This kind of magic is..." Charles laughed. "Storybook. The Old Tales, brought to life."

Derek let out a disbelieving breath. "It was..." He glanced at the closed double doors leading to the court. "It was the consequence. Part of the bargain I made to rescue Lydia."

"About that?" Charles turned from the painting and raised an eyebrow. "What exactly happened when you were in the sea? I thought you were off to rescue the love of your life?"

Derek nodded, a smile parting his lips. "Turns out she's the love of Alyana's life and... I don't think I've ever felt for someone the way those two feel for each other." He cocked his head. "I don't know that I ever will."

They stood in silence for a moment. Derek's mind was a jumble. Fragments of thoughts, idea, plans that he could never have imagined before the sea witch's magic had changed everything.

"Really though," he said.

Charles jerked out of his own revere of thoughts.

"You're sure I haven't ruined your life?"

Charles' laugh echoed along the marble floor. "Brother, I've..." He sucked in a breath, the smile on his lips one

Derek hadn't seen in a long time. "I've kept something from you to spare you concern. Keep you from your own anxiety."

Derek frowned and, when Charles didn't continue, he raised an eyebrow.

"Well." Charles swung away from him, digging his hands into his pockets and striding toward the door. "You had to marry first, and I didn't want you to be rushed. You've been engaged for a decade, but actually marrying her..." He shook his head. "I knew you weren't ready. Even if I was."

Derek's jaw dropped. He hurried forward, catching up to his brother and smacking his shoulder. "What do you mean, if you were?"

"Watch it," Charles snickered. "I'm the crown prince now, remember?"

Derek rolled his eyes. "You... you're in love, brother?"

Charles' freckled cheeks reddened. "Yes."

"And you've been waiting to marry..."

"Waiting to bring it up with father until you and the Lady were wed, yes. I knew if I expressed interest, he'd rush you. I couldn't have that."

A weight lifted from Derek's chest. "So when you wanted to look at the map..."

Charles laughed. "She is close. Another ally, though not as wealthy as Lydia's kingdom, certainly what father would call a *prize*." He made a face. "And she loves me too." A soft smile replaced the scrunched-up lips.

"Charles... I'm so glad. So happy for you." He let out a soft chuckle. "Good thing I got this back."

He passed the ring, the one that had graced their mother's hand in every memory they shared of her, to his brother. Charles gazed at it for a long moment before pocketing it.

"Thank you." Charles sighed. "And what of you? Where will the second son go?"

Derek clapped a hand on his brother's shoulder as the two of them stepped out onto the stone steps leading to the palace gardens and then gates. "I need to see it, Charles. I need to see this kingdom of ours."

Charles nodded. "You're going to fall in love, brother. With the people, the land." He rubbed a hand across his face. "And when it comes time to actually run the thing, I expect you to come back to help."

Derek laughed. "Of course." He took the first few steps, his feet lighter than they'd ever been before. "You're the *crown prince* after all, you can always command me back."

Charles shook his head with a chuckle. "Be safe, brother. Write me."

"And you. Make sure to give me some travel time before the wedding."

Charles nodded, Derek made his way to the stables, and the two brothers parted for who knew how long.

Derek hesitated at the cliff. His horse was ready to go, shifting her head and stamping, anxious to release some energy. Rocks jutted from the water, far from him, but still visible.

"You handled that rather well."

The voice jolted him from his staring. His horse whinnied.

A hand to his chest to steady his heartbeat, he looked down at Symphonia back in her usual skin. The black spiderwebs surrounded her face, a little deeper in some spots. The crown was gone from her tangled hair, but her dress made of sails remained. Her yellow gaze met his as she gave him a lopsided grin.

"I didn't think you'd break the shell," she said.

"What will you do?" Derek asked. "A full year without bargains."

She shrugged. "I was going to ask the same. You're free now."

He chuckled. "So are you."

She nodded. The smile fell from her lips, replaced with longing that ached at his heart as she stared out at the fields before them. "It's been so long. Decades I think, or centuries… it's hard to keep track you know, living alone."

Derek shifted in his saddle, patting his horse. "We're headed for the northern mountains. I've heard there's a rare fungus there." He shrugged. "Good for potions, apparently."

The witch turned to look him head on. She raised an eyebrow.

Derek couldn't stop the smile creeping across his face. "It's a dangerous road. Would be good to have company... if you wanted to come, that is."

Symphonia's eyes glinted. She snapped her fingers and—with a loud whinny—a translucent horse made of water erupted from the sea and galloped up the shore to her side. She grasped for a set of seaweed reins and, as she took hold of them, they materialized into leather. A saddle, bridle, and bag also formed. As she hefted a leg over the mount, it too became real. A cream-colored beast of flesh and blood.

She glanced at him as she shifted in the seat, gripping the reins and stretching her neck. "I thought you'd never ask."

With a whooping yell, she took off. Her horse bolted for the road. Derek's mare shifted again, snorting.

"All right," he chuckled. "Let's go."

They kicked up onto the path.

Derek breathed in deep, watching the sun begin its dip toward the horizon. A song picked up on the wind. A jaunty melody in a haunting tone. He hurried to catch up, to better hear the witch sing as they began their journey.

Acknowledgements

Thank you for reading!!

This was such an interesting story to write, but I never thought I'd publish it in long form. Thanks to the readers who wanted this in paperback and told me to do it!

Thanks to Tracey, cover artist extraordinaire, amazing friend, and wonderful supporter. I can't imagine my life without you.

Thank you, Sissy, for telling me to make it gay. You're a thousand percent right, it made for a much better story.

If you've enjoyed this story, please consider leaving a short review! They help a ton and make a big difference. Check out my other works at chlyn.com. And keep an eye out, this is just one of the Old Tales...

www.ingramcontent.com/pod-product-compliance
Lightning Source LLC
Chambersburg PA
CBHW061540310726
48972CB00008B/2548